ZOOMY ZOOMY

improv games and
exercises for groups

Hannah Fox

Tusitala Publishing

Zoomy Zoomy: Improv games and exercises for groups
Copyright © Hannah Fox 2010

Tusitala Publishing
137 Hasbrouck Road
New Paltz, NY 12561
USA

www.tusitalapublishing.com

Cover and interior photos by the author
Author photo by Matthew Fried
Cover and book design by WordGraphics

ISBN: 978-0-9642350-8-3

Printed in the United States of America.

For the late Augusto Boal,
beloved teacher and innovator, who continues to animate the world
with his presence and games.

And for my sister Maddy,
an inspiration in writing this book.

CONTENTS

PROLOGUE

Playing and learning

In these pages are all the theatre exercises that I've learned first hand as a student or made up on the spot as an instructor over the past 26 years. These games create a space for us to play together and connect with our joy; they also develop imagination, confidence, critical thinking, trust, connection and understanding within groups. And they continually reinvent themselves; I have played these games, as you might have, over and over again, and each time I play them, the parameters are refreshed and the experience is new. This is the luminous nature of improvisation, and the gift and wisdom of the present moment.

I was four years old when my parents first created Playback Theatre, a form of improv based on life stories. So jumping around a room making funny noises and faces has always been a familiar mode of behavior for me. When I was twelve I joined the Arts Community Youth Theatre in New Paltz, NY, directed by Steve and Carole Ford. I was a member until I graduated from high school. It was a creative outlet for sure, challenging and exciting, but more importantly, this assorted group of young people assembled together (and sometime adult actors from the community who joined our cast) to make theatre was a family. Steve and Carole asked me back on college breaks to assistant direct, which I was thrilled to do. It was here in the youth theatre that I had my first taste of how playing these physical and imaginative group games instantly creates community connection. I continued to teach theatre/group building workshops throughout my college and post-graduate career to earn a living—and never stopped playing these games. From 1995 to 2000 I created a youth theatre for teenage girls in Eugene, Oregon. In this theatre young women were empowered to write scenes and monologues based on issues in their lives. We devised original shows and toured them around the state. After I returned to New York I continued the work with young women, starting the 92 St. Y Youth Theatre, sponsored by Eve Ensler. I now teach theatre and dance at a small liberal arts college. In my youth theatre work as well as in the classes I teach now, these games and exercises are essential building blocks.

Some of these exercises are the very ones I learned from Steve and Carole all those years ago; others I have picked up along the way from other great teachers across the globe. The rest are originals I have made up, or variations on the theme. Many of the exercises I have learned from someone else I have adapted or embellished in some way, or sometimes renamed. I have tried my best to credit the person from whom I have learned a particular game. If I have taken something from someone and not given proper credit, please email me and I will correct my mistake! My intention has been to be as respectful as possible in this process.

It is the nature of theatre games to transform and change shape as they pass through hands and cultures and decades. Theatre games stay alive via the oral tradition, through action. Who knows what the "true original" is any longer or where or when it was conceived? (I imagine many of these exercises can probably be traced back to Viola Spolin.) What I do know after relying on these games for so long is that they work. These games inspire laughter, spontaneity, ensemble building, physical and vocal expression, concentration, self-discovery/reflection, self-esteem, and, ultimately, I believe, good health. They get adults, and teenagers too, *playing* again, which is no small feat. I wrote down these activities on paper (finally) because students and colleagues have repeatedly asked me to. My hope is that *Zoomy Zoomy* will serve as a resource for anyone who works with groups as well as encourage us all to keep playing.

As Playback Theatre is a central method that I teach and perform (with my New York City based theatre company Big Apple Playback Theatre), I will steer the conversation in that direction sometimes. On page tk you'll find warm up sequences for specific Playback forms.

In my work, I also readily pull from Theatre of the Oppressed (Augusto Boal), Viewpoints (Ann Bogart), Action Theatre (Ruth Zaporah), Motion Theatre (Nina Wise), Psychodrama (J.L. and Zerka Moreno), and Contact Improvisation (Steve Paxton et al) and so warm up activities from these techniques appear in the book as well. Essentially, I have written down everything that I use and find effective in building an ensemble and teaching performance skills.

How to use this book*

I have divided the games into categories: *Openers, Name Games, Physical warm up, Vocal warm up, Team-building games, Mapping/ Sociometry, Longer Activities*, and *Closing Activities.* You can read through the book in sequence or just pick and choose what sections or exercises are useful to you at the time. Following the games and exercises there are further resources you might find useful.

What is written on the pages of this book is not sacred; feel free to pick activities apart, add, subtract, expand, deflate, conflate, omit, riff on, and run with what you find in any direction that serves.

The art of teaching games

Teaching a theatre game to a group has its own skill set. It is an

---

* *Zoomy Zoomy* is not a teaching manual. It's essentially a list of theatre games, as the subtitle suggests. It is designed to be a resource for people who may already know something about teaching and who are looking for ideas for more activities. Teaching theatre is an oral tradition—you can't learn it from a book!

intuitive art first and foremost. One has a "lesson" but to find a satisfying flow and groove with a group, we need to tap into our felt sense. It is also true that the teaching happens in both directions: from teacher to student and from student to teacher. In the end, as Spolin says, it is each person's own *experience* that becomes the main instructor, or "informer." In addition to tapping our intuition, there are other important considerations. Each warm up has an *objective*. There is a reason for using a particular activity at a particular time--we are not pulling games out at random only because they are fun. A good facilitator stays attuned to the group's pulse and rhythm at all times; in other words, she *listens* to what the collective need is while keeping in sight the session's curriculum objective or main lesson. It is like the captain of a ship whose destination is charted but who has to navigate through ocean waters and various weather conditions to get to the distant shore. In addition to curriculum, for every class or workshop there will be considerations about group size, demographics, skill level, energy level, stage of the group's development, and time constraints when choosing the appropriate warm ups and games. Here is a list of nine factors I consider important when facilitating a group or workshop—whether a one- or two-hour workshop, a five-day training or a multi-week college class.

PLAN AHEAD

I find it crucial to come into a session with a game plan, a sequence of activities that has logic and reasoning and that leads up to a main lesson. This kind of lesson planning takes some time and careful thinking, but I find when I prepare and have a solid outline when I walk into the classroom or workshop space, the day has a clear aim and is that much more successful (and satisfying for the students).

STAY FLEX

Bring a plan but be prepared to abandon it! As important as it is to have a plan or an outline, it is as essential to remain flexible to the needs of the group at any given moment. You may have planned to start the day with a tag game outside but then in the morning either a) it is raining or b) the students are exhausted and need something more low key. Or you may have constructed a great sequence of warm ups aimed at a main activity but an unexpected discovery is made by the students in one of the warm up games which inspires the group to move in another direction, which, in the end, turns out to be much more meaningful and instructive than the original plan. Or perhaps the group is stumbling over a certain principle or is moving much slower than expected. You may need to pull a diction exercise or trust building exercise from your back pocket and work on that for the afternoon instead of what you planned. As the guide, it is necessary to stay open to these last minute changes. In this way, in leading groups, one needs to "go with the flow;" facilitation is an improvisation in itself.

WHY THIS GAME NOW?

How do we open up a session? When do we pull out a tag game? When is it the right moment to stop, sit and talk? What is the right last activity to engage in before you end the day? Each game serves a purpose and warms up a different muscle. A tag game energizes a group. A blindfold exercise creates focus within the group, wakes up the senses, and builds trust. A sound and movement exercise brings us out of our analytical brain and activates a more primal part of the brain (and also warms us up for *Fluid Sculptures*). A vocal warm up prepares us to speak clearly and project our voices on stage. Many of the circle games, like *Zip Zap Zop* or *Bunny Bunny*, function as focusers as well as team-building exercises. Again, it is good to think through your sequence of games in terms of your main learning objective for the day, and ask yourself: what am I warming the group up *to*? You also want to consider the size, age, and readiness of the group in your game selection. Again, at times, you will completely depart from the plan you have written down and introduce a game on a whim because you sense it is the best next step for the group.

FIT TO SIZE

Hopefully, you have an idea of the group size (number of people) before you enter the room, as planning a workshop for 10 is much different than for 20 or 50 or 100 or even 6. Some exercises work for big groups and not smaller groups, and vice versa. One needs a critical mass of at least 6 bodies to execute many of the games listed in this book effectively. You need a certain level of energy in the room and enough "clay" to work with. If you have a large group you may have to introduce the game to the whole group, select some students to demonstrate, and then split up into small groups to play. For instance, *Zoomy Zoomy* or *1-20-1* or *Yes* do not work very well with more than 18 people, so you would want to divide up into smaller groups of 10 or 12. Games like *Walk/Stop* or *Yes, Let's* work fine with a big group (50 or more).

SETTING IT UP

I know what it is like to be in a class when an instructor is introducing a game and the rules / parameters of the activity are not explained clearly. You go into the game having no idea of what is expected or how it works and it is frustrating! Take time to set up the game clearly: *What are the rules or guidelines? What is the objective?* You may need to repeat the key instructions to make sure everyone has heard and understood. Talk slowly, clearly and loud enough for everyone to hear. Leave room for questions and clarifications. If you have non-native speakers in the group, make sure they understood the instructions. Say the essentials but try not to go on for too long. After too many lengthy explanations students can get tired or shut down: less talk, more action! You may also need to do a short demonstration of the game to supplement the verbal explanation.

HANDS ON/ HANDS OFF

Every person has her or his own leadership style. However, it is always a choice how "hands on" (or directive) you want to be with each activity and with the group as a whole. You can choose to be in the role of coach throughout a game, chiming in often with words of encouragement and with clarifications, or you can choose to play more of a witness role and sit back and watch the process once you have introduced a game. I find that I do both. There are times that I cheerlead and participate in an activity and other times I step back and allow the group to guide itself. The group really is the main teacher in the room. How involved a facilitator is once the game has started depends on the exercise; it depends on the group; sometimes it depends on how tired I am. I think it is important to be present and vigilant as a facilitator at all times, but also to allow the group to breathe, stumble and discover things on its own. You may be someone who needs to practice more hands-off moments, or maybe the opposite, but either way, I suggest you use both approaches in your workshops.

WISDOM IN GROUP REFLECTION

I find the work deepens considerably when you leave time to debrief exercises. Perhaps not every activity but certainly the more involved ones. It is enriching and educational for the whole group to hear about people's experiences while participating in the game. Very often, profound revelations and insights are shared by group members. It is here in the post-activity discussion that these games become more than just opportunities for play; the discoveries made while playing them connect beyond the theatre context to life learning. It's also useful for people to understand consciously *why* we are doing a particular activity in the classroom. It is in the debrief process afterwards that a student can reflect on *why* this game was chosen over another, *what* skills we are intending to build, and *how* the experience has affected him/her.

AGREEMENTS AND EXPECTATIONS

Don't lose track of time. Stay on top of the clock. When did you agree to stop? How much time is left in the day or class; do you have enough time to delve into the next activity? How much time do you need for the final activity? I think being punctual (for both the facilitator and students)—starting and ending on time (within a healthy margin!)—is good form. In the "real" world, certainly in the theatre industry, if you are not on time, you can lose your job. Punctuality is an aspect of the discipline and work ethic needed to be a good performer. It is also a form of respect--for each other and for the work. And, finally, start and end times are an agreement that you made together as a community. Now, if you start five minutes late or will need to spill a little over time, and this is understood by the group, no worries!

TAKE NOTES

You probably do this already, but make notes as you go along (or directly after the class or workshop) about what worked and what didn't. This is valuable information that can ultimately save you lots of time. There have been plenty of times that I thought I would remember key points next time but when the workshop rolls around again, it is all a vague wash. Take a few minutes to *write your thoughts down while they're fresh*--and remember where you stored the notes. (You can write them right in this book if you want!) This way you do not have to keep reinventing the wheel.

A final word

We play theatre games to have fun, to tap the imagination, to warm up our bodies, to role-play, to develop skills, to build trust within the group. Over the last several years I have used these games for an additional purpose: to effect social change. When my company goes into a juvenile delinquent rehabilitation facility to conduct weekly theatre workshops, we are teaching the young people skills, but more importantly, we are creating an opportunity for this marginalized population to be seen and heard. We are offering them a chance to feel powerful, funny, smart, in control of their universe, even if for just an hour and a half. We also use these games as a tool for exploring issues of racism, sexism, homophobia, and other forms of oppression.

It is this deeper layer and thrust of the work that especially motivates me these days.

OPENERS

Atama/ Abaku/ Aberine

Whole group

I picked this up in West Africa. It is a call and response clap/chant generally used to focus a group. The caller says "ataMA" and the response from the group is one clap. When the caller says "aBAku," the clap response is three even claps. When the caller says "aberinE" (pronounced a-bear-i-NAY), the response is: 4 pairs of quick claps or 8 short, quick claps: 1/2, 3/4, 5/6, 7/8. The caller can mix these up in any manner she wants and the group needs to be ready with the appropriate clap response.

2 minutes.

Angel/nemesis

Whole group

This is a classic Boal exercise that is also called "Protector/Enemy" or "Friends and enemies." Everyone in the circle (minus the facilitator) secretly chooses someone else in the circle to be his or her "angel." I usually ask people to put their hand on their hip when they have chosen. Next people choose a second/different person to be their "enemy." I ask people to put their hand on their other hip after they have made this second choice. I always add the caveat that these are random choices for this moment—"nothing personal!"

Next the facilitator explains that at the word "Go," everyone must keep their "angel" between himself and his or her chosen "enemy" or else (they will be struck by lightning, my words). Afterwards, I usually invite people to go up to their "angel" and give them a high five (or hug), and then go up to their "enemy" and give them a high-ten! (Augusto Boal)

5 minutes.

Shakeout 8,7,6

Whole group

This is a group activity to energize and warm up the body. Everyone raises her/his right arm and shakes it vigorously while counting down in rapid speed from 8 to 1. Then left arm, then right leg, then left leg. Repeat with right arm counting down from 7 to 1 (then left arm, right leg, and left leg). Continue to count down (6-1, 5-1, 4-1, 3-1, 2-1, 1-1) while shaking your limbs vigorously. Everybody is shaking and counting down. Naturally, you can count up instead of down if you wish.

5 minutes.

Footprints

Whole group

As the group combs the space, invite people to imagine that they have dipped their feet into a beautiful color of paint and are putting their "footprints" down all over the floor, making their "mark" as it were. The goal is to change the surface of the floor into a colorful mosaic of everyone's footprints.

3 minutes.

Start/stop

Whole group

Group walks around the room—not aimlessly, but with purpose, not following any pattern but in all directions and moving towards the empty spaces. When one person stops, everyone stops. When someone else feels the impulse to walk again, the whole group begins to move again, starting and stopping together as a unit, as if the group were one insect with many legs. At some point the facilitator can ask everyone to form an image or shape spontaneously with their bodies (individually), paying attention to levels and spatial relationship to other actors; and then come back into neutral when the walking begins again.

5 minutes.

Mix and mingle

Whole group

To recorded music or a tambourine, the whole group moves/dances through the space. When the music stops, everyone finds a partner and answers the questions listed below. The facilitator gives a minute or two for each partner to answer the question and then starts up the music again. When the music stops, people find a new partner and respond to the next question. Examples of questions: What do you like to eat for breakfast? Favorite kind of music? What is a fear that you have? What is something you feel passionate about?

5 minutes.

Body part greeting

Partners

To music, live or recorded, the actors move about the room. The facilitator cues them when to stop and find a partner (if there is an odd number, it is fine to have a group of three). Then the facilitator instructs the participants which body part to "say hello" to each other with: "Greet this person with your elbows." And the next time: "Find a new partner and say hello with your knees." Feet, bellies, rear-ends, shoulders, etc. Touch is optional.

5 minutes.

Sound & movement

Whole group

An opening circle improv game that we often start with in a Playback Theatre workshop. Someone offers a spontaneous sound and movement. It may or may not illustrate how he is feeling. The group echoes back his sound and movement. Encourage using the whole body.

Variations:

1. Each player says his or her name, then creates a Sound and Movement. The group echoes back the name and sound and movement,

2. The actor creates a movement as she says her name. The group repeats the name plus movement (there is no "sound" in this variation).

3. Instead of repeating the name and movement each time, you can let 3 or 4 people go and then go back to the first person, asking the group to repeat and remember each person's name-and-movement as a string. You can go back to the first person each time as you collect more people in your string or continue to collect and "review" 4-5 people at a time.

(Duration depends on group size: in a large group this can take a long time!)

Impulse

Whole group

Someone in the circle makes a spontaneous sound and movement and passes (gives) it to the person directly next to him who instantly transforms it into her own sound and movement and passes it on to the next person, so spontaneous sound and movement is passed around the circle like a wave or a current of lightning. The impulse should move fast, therefore the sound and movements should be quick, one beat or "syllable" long. After the impulse has been established it can move in either direction, and then even across the circle.

2 minutes.

Impulse plus

Whole group

In this version, someone offers a sound and movement, which moves around the circle (everyone repeats this sound and movement). When the gesture gets back to the first person, she repeats it and, without missing a beat, the next person offers a new sound and movement, which circulates around the circle until it reaches the originator—who repeats it—and which is followed by a new gesture by the next person. You want the sounds and gestures to be "one beat" or one syllable long so that they can move around the circle swiftly. You don't want to do this with an especially large circle (over 15) because it can take too much time. Another option, with a large group, would be to split up into smaller groups.

Depends on group size; usually 5 minutes.

1 minute check-in

Whole group

Stand in a circle. In turn, each person gets one minute (timed) to share how s/he is doing. (Nina Wise)

Line up

Small groups

Divide the group into teams of four or five and have them line up in rows. Within each row each person stands behind another, and the rows are side by side. Then you give them categories and each team has to line up according to the prompts given—before the other teams. Once the group feels they have accomplished the task (properly lined up), the members sit down. First team sitting down "wins". For all of these there is no talking—non-verbal communication only! Some categories: hair length; birthdays (January downstage); first letter of last name; age.

10 minutes.

Hand check-in

Partners or whole group in circle

The hands can be very expressive and act like puppets. Each person in turn "checks in" (describes his/her day or week) using her/his hands. You are trying to convey the essence and emotion of your story as well as action/plot (the story can be portrayed literally or in more of an abstract way).

Each check in about 1 minute.

Rose and thorn

Partners or whole group in circle

Everyone is invited to share a "rose" (something positive about their current life) and a "thorn" (a conflict or challenge from their current life) aloud with the rest of the group. Usually, each person shares both, the rose and the thorn, before the next person goes.

Depends on group size; usually about 2 minutes each person.

Story of my name

Whole group in circle

In turn, everyone shares her full name and tells what they know of why they were called what they were. Some people don't know, but many names have interesting family stories attached. (Zerka Moreno)

Depends on group size; usually 2-4 minutes each person.

Urban ball

Whole group

Stand in a circle. Facilitator has a piece of paper crumpled up into a ball. The object of the game is for the group to keep the ball in the air for as many swats as it can, counting together as a group when someone hits the ball. When the ball falls onto the floor the group goes back to "one". You cannot hit it twice in a row and it is critical that the group cheers every time someone drops the ball, saying: "Yay, good job! Nice try!!" so that it stays more about team spirit and less about counting to a high number. I find this is best with groups of 7-10. If needed, break large group up into smaller groups. (Helen White)

5-10 minutes.

The cross and the circle

Whole group

This is a fun, quick whole group warm up to test to see who is awake. Ask people to draw a circle in the air with their right pointer finger. Then ask them to draw a cross or plus sign with their left pointer finger. Then ask them to "draw" them simultaneously, the circle and the square. It is much like patting your head and rubbing your tummy. This is great to do at the very beginning of a session, or sometimes we even do it at the beginning of a Playback performance, after the opening. In that case it serves as a good ice-breaker. (Augusto Boal)

3 minutes.

Partner interviews

Partners

This is a meet-and-greet exercise for the first day of a training or class. Everybody finds a partner and "interviews" the other person answering 3 assigned questions, in addition to finding out this person's name. The 3 questions might include: *What is a hobby you have? What is something you are passionate about? What is a fear you have? What is your favorite food? Where is a place you would like to travel in this world and why? What is something that makes you unique?* You can cater the questions to any theme the group may be exploring. After both parties answer the questions, you reconvene as a whole group in a circle and everybody introduces her/his partner and shares their 3 bits of information.

Sometimes I have people embody or act out their report back instead of just speaking the answers. (If it is a large group you many have people pick just one or two of the three facts to share with the whole group instead of all three.)

Interviews 5 minutes.

Name Games

Juggling

Whole group

Need 4 or 5 balled-up pairs of (clean!) socks or
tennis balls

Someone in the circle gently throws a ball or pair of
socks to someone else in the circle, first saying their
name. This person catches the ball by looking at the
thrower and saying "Yes." (A most essential mantra for
improvisation.) The new person with the ball looks at
someone else across the circle, says her name, and gently
throws the ball. The catcher makes eye contact with the
thrower and says "Yes". Each catcher throws the ball
to someone new, and eventually the last person throws
the ball back to the first person, thereby establishing a
pattern, which is repeated again. (In other words, you are
throwing the ball to the same person you threw to in the
first round.)

After a rhythm and a level of comfort are established
with the throwing pattern, the facilitator can introduce
a second ball (and then a third, fourth, etc.) into the
mix, sticking to the same pattern. Eventually you can
eliminate the "yes" part of the dialogue, saying to the
group that it is implied in the moment of eye contact
(which should not be eliminated). I always preface
this game by saying that if a ball drops it is NO BIG
DEAL—no one dies, no one cares—just pick it up
and jump back in the game. Once all balls are in play, I
usually yell out, "We're juggling! It is this kind of group
rhythm we want to maintain when we are on stage
together."

Depends on group size; generally 8-10 minutes.

Bubbly Brenda

Whole group

In a circle, the first person thinks of an adjective that can come before (or after) her name that has the same beginning sound as her first name (Amusing Ann, Boisterous Bob, Cat-loving Caroline) and does a movement with her body as she shares her alliterated name out-loud. The group repeats it back. You can move around the circle one person at a time, or, like the Name and Movement game above, you can work accumulatively, doing a few at a time and continuing to return back to the beginning each time.

Depends on group size.

Three times

Whole group

Someone volunteers to go into the middle of the circle. The person who is "It" in the center must say someone else's name in the circle three times in a row before that person says the center person's name once. So, if I were in the center, I would attempt to call out someone else's name in the circle 3X: "Mario, Mario, Mario!" before Mario stays "safe" by saying my name once before I get to the third repetition of his name. If I manage to say "Mario, Mario, Mario!" before he says my name (just once) then he is out and comes into the center, and I return to the circle. (Helen White)

5 minutes.

Physical
Warm Up

Tag games serve as great energizers and physical warm ups. Play tag games outside whenever possible.

Fox/rabbit

Whole group

One person volunteers to be the Fox and another person the Rabbit. The other actors pair up, face each other, grab hands or wrists, and make "rabbit holes" with their arms. The Fox chases the Rabbit trying to tag him. The way the Rabbit can be safe is to go into a rabbit hole. When she does this she "bumps" one of the rabbit hole people out by standing in front of them and replacing that side of the rabbit hole. The rabbit hole person who was bumped out becomes the new Rabbit, whom now the Fox has to chase and try to catch. If the Fox succeeds in tagging the Rabbit, the Rabbit now becomes the Fox and tries to catch the old Fox (who is now the Rabbit).

5 minutes.

Bump

Whole group

Same concept as F&R except instead people are standing one in front of the other, both facing the same way. Someone is "It" and this person chases and tries to catch someone else. The way the chased person can be safe is to join the front of a standing couple and bump the back person out--who then is chased by "It". If you're caught you become It!

5 minutes.

Goblins/witches/giants

Whole group, two teams

This is a more complicated tag game than the others described. There are three options that the groups choose from each round: Giants, Witches, and Goblins. Each of these characters has power over another: the Giants smush the Goblins; the Witches put spells on the Giants; and the Goblins tickle under the Witches' skirts (don't ask). Before you start it is fun to have the whole group practice embodying these characters, setting what each looks like, and reviewing who has power over whom.

Each group then huddles up and decides together which of the characters they will be as a group. When both teams have decided, they meet in the middle and everyone chants: "Goblins, Witches, and Giants, oh my! 1, 2, 3" and quickly become their characters. If one group becomes Giants and the other Goblins then the Giants chase the Goblins back to their home base trying capture as many as they can. If you reach your home base you are safe, if captured you join the other team. If one group became Witches and the other Goblins then the Goblins would chase the Witches trying to tag and capture as many Witches as possible. If both groups become the same character it is a free for all and everyone tries to scramble back to their home base before being caught.

For each round the two respective groups decide what they're going to be and return to the center in a line to begin the chant together.

5 minutes.

Head to toes

Whole group

Ideally to music, participants are guided through an improvisational dance warm up with the facilitator calling out various body parts for the dancer-actors to focus on. Initiate movement through space with your feet. Let your feet talk. Let them tell a story… now with your knees… your hips…your belly… your back… shoulders… elbows… hands… chest… head… nose… Now, your whole body, head to toes… let it move freely through space—in the air, on the floor; explore different levels… different rhythms and textures… perhaps your exploration may bring you close to another dancer … You want to leave a minute or two for each body part and then 2-5 minutes for the final bit in which the dancers move the whole body freely with possible interaction.

10 minutes.

Body part vowels

Whole group

This is a fun and quick physical warm up. Similar to Head to Toes, this time, however, participants are "drawing" the alphabet vowels (A, E, I, O, U and Y) in space. The facilitator calls out a different body part for each vowel. Draw an "A" with your knees. Draw an "E" with your tailbone. Draw an "I" with your arms. Draw an "O" with your shoulders. And so on.

5 minutes.

So you think you can dance!

Whole group in circle or teams

Circle:

A volunteer in the circle creates four beats of choreography on the spot, staying in their place in the circle—which the rest of the circle practices. Then another volunteer from the circle adds on four more beats of choreography. The whole group practices all eight counts. Then a third person adds on, etc. until there is a small dance that everyone knows. You can add the element of the African dance "circle" at the end of the choreographed group piece in which people can volunteer to dance free-style in the middle of the circle while the rest of the group claps and vocalizes.

Teams:

In teams of 2-5, groups create a short piece of choreography. Ideally everyone in the group contributes a move or an idea. The dance teams rehearse and then show their dance to the other teams.

10 minutes.

Dowel dance

Whole group

Need lightweight dowels, one per pair

Each person finds a dance partner. One 2-3 foot wooden dowel is assigned to each duet. To music, the partners create an improvisational dance with the dowel connecting them. They can use different body parts to hold the dowel up between them, but they try not to let the dowel ever drop to the floor. (Christian Penny and Bev Hosking)

5 minutes.

Relay race

Teams

This is a fun, quick way to warm up a group: a good old-fashioned relay race! Divide groups up into teams of four or five and announce the events. Some examples are: sprinting forward and then backward; hopping; the frog (hands/feet/hands/feet); rolling; leaps; the waltz (two people at a time); piggy-back (two people). After you announce the various legs of the race, the teams designate who will be going for each part. For each "event" the designated person will cross the room and back. Facilitator starts everyone off. Once you are done with your leg, you tag the next "runner" and sit down. When everyone has gone the team sits down. First team sitting down, wins.

5 minutes.

Empty Vessel

Whole group

Everyone stands in a circle. One person volunteers to go into the middle and begin a repetitive, rhythmic sound and dance movement. Everyone in the circle mimics the sound and movement (optional). The person in the center chooses someone from the periphery and moves his rhythmic sound/movement over to that person. They face each other dancing in unison and then they exchange places and this new person moves back into the center changing the original sound into something different, allowing the transformation process to happen organically. This new repetitive, rhythmic movement is done in the center for 30 seconds or so and then this person selects a new person on the periphery to "give" the movement to. They have a moment dancing in unison face to face and then change places. Depending on the size of the circle you can play this game until everyone has had a chance in the center or you can cut it off after 10 minutes or so. There is a continual stream of sounding and moving until the game is over.

10 minutes.

Basketball

Whole group

In this quick, fun, physical warm up, you simply get a rigorous game of air basketball going around the room (court). Two teams may or may not emerge, but there is dribbling, passing and basket shooting.

2 minutes.

Maniac

Whole group

Everyone runs in place rigorously, knees up, singing the chorus of "Maniac" from the movie Flashdance ("She's a maniac, maniac on the floor; and she's dancing like she's never danced before"). Then, together, everyone either drops to the floor and does 10 push ups or does 10 jumping jacks, counting out loud. This whole sequence is repeated a few times.

5 minutes.

Squeegee

Partners

This is essentially a massage exercise. One partner stands behind the other with his hands on his partner's shoulders. Both parties breathe together for a beat or two and then the back person (the massage therapist or squeegee) massages the back of the front person, and then squeezes down the arms, hips, legs, gives a good squeeze to the ankles, and then back up again, finishing with his hands back on the shoulders for a moment of stillness. You can go into trust falls from here or just change roles.

6 minutes.

Pass the face

Whole group

This is a great exercise to warm up the face. Everyone stands in a circle. One person starts by making an exaggerated face to the circle (funny, grotesque, shocking, angry, sad, happy, etc.). She then turns to her right (or left) and that person mimics the face—so for a moment there is a mirror reflection. This second person then turns his head back to the center, facing the circle, with the face he was just "given" and lets the "mask" transform to something new. Once he feels settled into this new face or mask, he turns to the next person and passes the face on.

Depends on circle size; about 20 seconds each person.

Circle sit

Whole group

Everyone stands in a close circle standing in front of each other. You need to be situated in a way that if the person in front of you were to sit down your lap could provide him a seat. When everyone is close enough and angled correctly, at the facilitator's cue, everyone sits down at the same time slowly. If lined up properly everyone should land on a lap and be comfortable and stable. On cue, everyone stands up again. Sometimes the group successfully sits and stands; other times everyone ends up on the ground—either way is fun!

2 minutes.

Trust fall

Partners

This is a classic theatre trust building exercise. I find it essential for helping actors to face fears, build ensemble and also get to know and get comfortable with each others' physical weight in case a lift or carry is required down the line! One actor stands a foot or so behind another actor in a wide stance with one leg in front of the other. She puts her hands a couple of inches away from the "faller's" back. When she is ready and is in a steady position to support weight, she says "Go," which is the cue for the front actor to fall back into her hands.

The faller should try to fall like a plank of wood in one piece—shoulders, hips and ankles all lined up—rolling onto his heels and allowing his feet to come off the ground. If the faller and catcher feel comfortable they can take it to the next step. The catcher moves back a few inches and now catches the faller under the arms. If able, the catch can take the faller all the way, or almost, to the floor. It's helpful to have partners with similar body size.

10 minutes.

Trust fall circle

Small groups

This is a great trust fall exercise for groups after a foundation is built. Form circles of 8-10 people.

Someone stands in the middle of circle with her arms criss-crossed over her chest and her eyes closed. The people on the periphery of the circle stand shoulder to shoulder with a one foot in front of the other (to create sturdy bases of support). When ready the center person begins to fall in any direction, keeping her feet in one spot, as a pivot point. She is then gently, carefully passed around the circle, forward, backward, sideways. It is best that more than one person "catch" at once, i.e. four or six hands rather than just two. The experience should be fluid and peaceful for the faller; she should feel like she is in good hands!

10-12 minutes.

Contact Improv sequence

Partners

Contact Improvisation is a terrific form to help actors tune into each other, to practice non-verbal listening and body sensing, to build a physical weight-sharing vocabulary within a group, and to build ensemble. There are specific skills, lifts, falls and rolls that can be taught as well as opening up the space for a contact jam or open dance. The following is a simple contact stretch sequence that I use with groups as a warm up—either for more contact or to prepare for other work. Naturally, you can use part of or add to this series.

I suggest going through the sequence with a couple of friends before you lead this in a workshop!
Begin with partners facing each other—hands on each other's shoulders, breathing and tuning in.

Both dancers bring their toes close to partner's toes and slide their hands out until they are grabbing wrists. I call this Leaning out into the Wind.

Slide hands to each other's shoulders again, move feet way out until each person's back is straight and feet are under hips. This should be a good hamstring stretch. I call this Bridge. Move from Wind to Bridge a few times.

Grab opposite wrists with just one arm, keeping the other arm free, and try to find a balance holding onto each other with just one hand, and maybe only one foot by taking the other foot off the ground momentarily. I call this Dangle.

Grab wrists again, straight arms and bending your knees together move tailbone towards the floor until both people are in a squat. This should feel good on your spine. I call this Tumbleweed.

Both people sit on the floor and turn back to back. One person extends his legs out long in front of him and the other person takes a gentle ride leaning her back into his as he leans his torso over towards his legs. This is a hamstring stretch for him and a heart opening stretch for his partner whose chest is now facing the sky. Reverse positions gently, fluidly, moving up and over like a seesaw. I call this Seesaw. You can continue on and repeat this motion with your knees bent and soles of the feet together in butterfly or move on.

Next, one person comes up into Table pose on her hands and knees. (If someone has sensitive knees or a recent knee injury, you may want to put something soft like a shirt under your knees or opt out.) The other person places his lower back on her buttocks/lower back area (the part that is supported by the knees- not the mid-back) and lies back into a backbend keeping his feet on the floor or finding a balance point and lifting his feet off the floor. If he is balancing the supported surface area of his partner she should feel no pain or discomfort.

This is called Over the Rainbow. Once he has had a good stretch he can gently peel his way back up OR (more advanced) he can gently slide down the other side until his head and hands reach the floor and scissor kick his legs over his head for a graceful walkover dismount. The facilitator can always serve as a spot. Partners change roles.

Sitting back to back once again, the partners latch elbows, step their feet into the floor (no socks!), press equally into each other's backs and try to stand up. The key is to press into each other as you straighten your knees.

Finally, one person acts as the oak tree standing solid and still and the other as the itchy grizzly bear and the bear gets a good scratch all over her furry back—up, down and all around—trying to scratch as much surface area as possible. Change roles.

5 Rhythms

Whole group

In this warm up you put on some groovin' music and dance through Gabriele Roth's five rhythms: flowing, staccato, chaos, lyrical, stillness—possibly changing the music for each state. Each dancer interprets these different states for themselves with their own bodies. It is nice to do at least 2 minutes for each state. (Gabriele Roth)

10 minutes.

Star jumps

Whole group

Make a big standing circle. This game involves jumping and running across the circle. One person starts out running across the circle up to someone else. When she arrives the runner and the person now opposite from her jump together in the air arms and legs spread like a star. Then the runner takes the place of her star jump friend, and this person now runs across the circle, chooses someone else with whom to star jump in the air with; they switch places, etc. After the group gets the hang of it you can start a second star jump line going, and then a third and eventually a fourth, by adding runners. (Matt Chapman)

5 minutes.

Yoga

Yoga is an ancient physical and spiritual practice that focuses the mind and increases strength and flexibility in the body. If the facilitator is familiar with yoga, it can be a wonderful method for warming up performers. Even just five or ten minutes of sun salutations or stretching at the beginning of a session is beneficial in so many ways. I use yoga postures to warm up in almost all of my theatre classes as well as company rehearsals. Each actor stretching in silence on her/his own, listening to what her/his body needs, is also very useful. Our body is our main instrument as dance and theatre artists; it is essential to keep it strong, supple, and articulate. (To learn more about yoga, consult the many texts written about it or find a class in your town or city.)

5-10 minutes.

Authentic Movement

Partners

Authentic Movement is a profound warm up tool,

developed by Mary Starks Whitehouse in the 1950s, in which our deep, sometimes unconscious, impulses are expressed through movement. In authentic movement we move with our eyes closed in front of a witness. In this basic exercise people choose a partner and then decide who will first be the mover and who will be the witness. The movers choose a place to start in the room and assume a starting position (standing up, sitting, on the ground), closing their eyes. This is a very internal process—there are no expectations around how the mover should move—this is not a "dance", but instead a movement improvisation in which the mover is following her inner guide. This may mean that during the time allotted (3 minutes, 5 minutes, 10 minutes) she barely moves at all; or it may mean that at points her movement becomes frenetic, fast, and perhaps even takes her around the room.

The witness's job is to keep the mover safe by following her intently and intercepting if she comes close to bumping into another person or furniture. After the movement exploration is finished (often sounded by a bell) and the mover has opened her eyes, she is invited to talk about her experience to her witness. In return, the witness can reflect back what he saw, possibly even echoing back a specific movement. Then the mover and witness change roles.

The debrief component is important as this form can move people into a deep emotional landscape. (Mary Whitehouse)

Vocal Warm Up

For more detailed vocal warm ups Kristin Linklater's **Freeing the Natural Voice** *is a great resource.*

Tongue Twisters

Whole group

Everyone repeats the tongue twister as fast as possible:

Unique New York, Unique New York, You know I Need Unique New York

Red Leather, Yellow Leather, Blue Leather

Bu da ga, Pi ta ka

One minute per tongue twister.

Jaw opener

Whole group

Each person clasps his hands together and shakes them vigorously, opening up his mouth and saying "ah". This vigorous shaking of the hands should serve to separate the top jaw from the bottom jaw. (Note: hands are not touching jaw!)

30 seconds.

Gargoyle

Whole group

Invite everyone to contort their face, hands and bodies becoming grotesque and frightening gargoyle creatures while making hideous noises. This serves to warm up the muscles of the face, arms, and hands as well as stimulates the soft palate. I must add how cathartic it is to have permission to be so ugly. (Nina Wise)

30 seconds.

Hah kicks

Whole group

This exercise warms up the diaphragm muscle. In a circle, everyone puts their hands on their lower belly and expresses a loud "hah," loud enough to make their hands move up and down. The sound should be strong, from the gut. Then everyone moves together through the following sequence, cued by the facilitator. It works like a call and response chant. Facilitator: Right arm. Group: Hah! (with body action). You begin with your right arm and with a strong "hah" you throw your right arm away "across the circle". Next left arm, same thing: throw your left arm across the circle with a strong "hah." Repeat with right leg, left leg, head, tail, and "whole self".

4 minutes.

HahHahHah

Whole group, circle or pairs facing one another

I learned this diaphragmatic/vocal warm up in 4th grade in Susan Slotnick's dance class and still use it to this day! Standing in neutral, with your hand on your belly, you articulate a sharp, strong "hah" (your hand should move) 16 times, and then using your lungs to full capacity, you hold a "hum" for 16 counts. Without missing a beat, the group chants "hah" 8 times, and holds "hum" for 8 counts. You do the eights twice (each round equals 16). Next is 4 "hah's," hold "hum" for 4 counts (repeat 4's four times). 2 "hah's," hold "hum" for two (repeat 8 times). Finally, singles: "hah, hum, hah, hum, hah, hum" etcetera, for 16 times and you hold a final hum for as long as you can. (Susan Slotnick)

5 minutes.

Team-Building Games

Soundball

Whole group

In a circle an imaginary ball of sound is thrown around from person to person. One person mimes throwing the ball to another in the circle (making eye contact) with a spontaneous sound (not words). The person who "catches the ball" repeats the sound to the best of their ability, pulling the "sound" in toward their chest, then throws the ball to a new person with a new sound (which is repeated and then transformed, etc.) The goal is to get a nice game of catch going (catch/throw, catch, throw) and not leave too much time to think or prepare. Ideally your eyes don't go down as you catch and then throw the "ball." Experiment with all kinds of sounds—surprise yourself and the group!

Variations: Eventually you can expand the sounds to "sentences" (gibberish), which the catcher repeats, and then transforms as she throws the ball to someone else.

Leave out the repetition of the sounds or sentences, and just throw the ball with a sound (which is caught without repeating). This variation allows the rhythm to pick up and for a lively group conversation to ensue.

5 minutes.

Zip Zap Zop

Whole group

Another well-known game of which there are many variations. The variation I play is the word ZIP is passed around the circle to the RIGHT with a clap (again "giving" it to the person next to you with eye-contact)— this is done with energy and commitment. When that has been established, you introduce ZAP, which is passed

around to the LEFT with a clap. When the clap comes
to you, you can choose to pass ZIP to the right or ZAP
to the left. Finally, ZOP is sent across the circle (to
anyone but the person directly to your right or left. The
key principles in this game are energy, conviction, and
diction. A common variation of this game is to send the
Zip, Zap and Zop around the circle with an energetic
clap to anyone in the circle in any direction following the
sequence of "Zip" then "Zap" then "Zop" over and over as
fast as possible.

4 minutes.

Ya So Ba

Whole group

Another version of this game is called Ya So Ba. "Ya" is
passed to the right, "So" to the left, and "Ba" across the
circle. You can also use the second variation of Zip Zap
Zop with Ya So Ba. (Jason Agar)

5 minutes.

Power clap

Whole group

Everyone in the circle assumes a wide, steady tai chi
stance. One person begins by making eye contact with
the person next to her and synchronizing a clap with
that person. That person then pivots to the next person,
and claps with him. The clap is sent around the circle.
The goal is to create one clap with the people next to you
(you will be receiving and giving) while maintaining eye
contact. It requires concentration and rhythm. Once a
steady clap is circulating, the facilitator can introduce a

second clap and then a third. (Helen White)

5 minutes.

What are you doing?!

Whole group

Someone in the circle begins with a pantomime of some activity, such as riding a bike, writing a letter, or brushing her teeth. The person on her right says, "Lauren, what are you doing?!" Lauren continues to mime riding a bike but says something totally different (without missing a beat): "I'm digging a ditch." Therefore, her physicalization does not match her dialogue. The questioner responds by taking on the physical activity of what Lauren said and begins to mime digging a ditch. When the person on his right asks what he is doing, he continues to dig a ditch but says, "I'm flossing my teeth" (or something else equally unrelated to his physical action). Continue around the circle.

Depends on group size.

Pantomime

Whole group

A lively and fun opening activity (after names) for a new group. Each person in the circle takes a turn pantomiming a favorite hobby or passion and the rest of the group guesses out loud.

Depends on group size; generally 5 minutes.

Who is leading?

Whole group

One person goes out of the room. The group stands in

a circle and someone volunteers to be the "Leader." He begins a simple, repetitive motion with his body (not voice), e.g., stomping his feet or snapping his fingers and jumping up and down or waving his arms up in the air. The whole group imitates this motion. The person is invited back into the room into the center of the circle. She needs to decipher who is leading the motion. Whenever possible the "Leader" changes the movement, but only when the center person is not looking. The followers in the circle also must be careful not to give away the Leader by looking directly at him, especially when changes in the movement take place. The person in the middle gets three guesses to try to reveal the Leader's identity. (Viola Spolin: "Who Started the Motion")

5 minutes.

3 Irish duels

Partners

These are great fun and very energizing. The following are my nicknames. (In Boal's version the third duel is the knee-touch.)

On Guard!—Partners face each other with their right arm outstretched, like a fencing sword (pointer and middle finger long as the tip of the sword) and the other hand behind the back, palm out. At the facilitator's cue the goal is to tap your partner's open palm with your "sword" more times than she taps yours.

Toe Tap—Partners try to tap the tops of each other's feet with theirs as many times as possible. (Both partners should be either shoed or barefoot.)

One Foot—Both partners cross their arms across their chest and then lift one foot off the ground (bending the knee) and balance on the other foot. On the cue, the goal is to knock your partner off balance, forcing them to put their raised foot down. You play until the facilitator says "stop," seeing who knocks whom over the most. (Augusto Boal)

5 minutes.

Over the line

Partners

Another one of Augusto Boal's brilliant and simple warm ups. Partners face each other and designate an imaginary line between them. Then they take hold of each other's shoulders. At the cue "Go," each person tries to get his/her feet over the line by pushing into the other person. Whoever manages "cross the line" wins. (Augusto Boal: "Pushing Against Each Other")

2 minutes.

Embodiments

Whole group

In this exercise one gets to *be* a sandwich or a diamond necklace instead of holding one in his/her hand. The facilitator asks the group to walk around the room in neutral. Then she calls out an inanimate object or feeling or state (summer time, dirty sock, lightning storm, pollution, a deadline, fresh cup of coffee) and the group members become what has been called out, finding the shape, walk, face, sound or text that this thing might say—personifying the thing. After 10 seconds or so, the facilitator hits a drum or tambourine, and the group members let the action go, come back to neutral and wait until the next suggestion is made. Encourage people to stay on their feet. You can tailor the list of items to a particular theme you might be working with. You can also take suggestions from the group at a certain point, or divide the group in half and create an audience/witness.

10 minutes.

Environments

Whole group

This exercise offers students an opportunity to endow different physical environments. People begin to walk around the room in neutral. The facilitator calls out different environments one at a time, which the students explore in action. Students are paying specific attention to how their body posture and tempo change within each environment. The environments can be listed as a kind of sequential journey (like the following example) or in no particular sequence. Example: *It is just starting to rain; it is now pouring down rain—you are getting soaked; now the wind has picked up and you are stuck walking in a full fledged storm; you have now reached the canopy cover of the woods; the ground is a swamp which you have to cross; now you are out the other side of the swamp and woods, the rain has stopped and a very hot sun has emerged from behind the clouds; you come to a 4 ft river of very cold water that you must cross; now you have 5 more miles to go and it has become very hot and humid—over 100 degrees Fahrenheit; you have one more field to cross and for some reason it is littered with broken glass; you are almost across when a mad swarm of hornets start chasing you, etc.*

10 minutes.

Sound and movement conversation

Partners

This is a nonverbal conversation in sound and movement instead of words.

Person A starts the "conversation" by "saying something" to person B using sound and movement (using legs, arms, head, chest, hands, feet, tail, belly). A "speaks" or moves and sounds for about 30 seconds, then freezes in a shape. When A freezes, B responds in sound and movement, again saying a few "sentences" and then freezing. A and B continue on like this and have a lively conversation until the facilitator calls time.

5 minutes.

Sounder/mover

Partners

One person is the sounder and the other is the mover. The sounder creates a soundscape, exploring different qualities and textures of sound. The mover improvises movement to his partner's sonorous composition, using all of his limbs, the floor, etc. After 3 minutes or so the Mover and Sounder switch roles. This is a great vocal and physical warm up as well as a team-building activity. You can also do this in small groups and have more than one sounder and mover.

7 minutes

What is it?

Whole group

In a seated or standing circle, the facilitator passes around an object (masking tape roll, broom stick, ruler) which each member of the circle gets to "name" by showing how it is used. It can be anything but what the object actually is. For instance, a roll of tape might be one cheerio in a bowl of cheerios (the actor acts out eating breakfast cereal) or an earring. A broom might become an old person's cane or a big piece of corn on the cob, or a Q-tip! The goal is for the group to engage in a creative and physical brainstorm not repeat any answers. If your mind is blank you can say pass.

Depends on group size; generally 5 minutes.

Engagement ring

Whole group

Also an endowment game as well as a great way to brainstorm metaphorical uses for the Playback fabric. (In Playback Theatre there is often a collection of colorful pieces of fabric on stage, which the actors use intermittently throughout a performance to symbolize certain aspects of the story.) People pass a piece of fabric around the circle endowing it as different things (abstract not literal), such as: *tension between lovers, the lost engagement ring, family ties, someone's crippling guilt, the burden of a child (parent) on a parent (child), the light at the end of the tunnel, instrument of flirtation, someone's sharp tongue.* Each actor shows and then explains each idea. You can go around the circle a few times.

30 seconds each person.

Bunny Bunny

Whole group

In a circle someone starts out as the designated "Bunny". She pulls up her hands like paws and says

"Bunnybunnybunny" as fast as she can. The two people on either side hold up their arms making bunny ears for the "Bunny Bunny" person. Together the three of them make an image of a bunny. After a few seconds, the person saying "bunny bunny" passes it to someone else in the circle with a pointed clap and says "Bunny!" as she passes (making eye contact with the receiver). The person being passed the "bunny" picks it up as quickly as possible pulling up her/his paws and saying "Bunnybunnybunny" over and over as the people on either side make the ears. Those who make a mistake are "out" and leave the circle. They can watch or become hecklers. (Enid Lefton/Wymprov)

4 minutes.

Charlie's Angels

Group

This game has many variations! Someone stands in the middle and calls out a command—"Charlie's Angels!" "Palm Tree!"—while pointing at someone. The person they are pointing at becomes the middle part of a three-person stage picture. The goal for all three people (the middle person and two people on either side) is to hit the picture instantly. If someone gets the wrong picture or takes too long getting there, they are "out" and become the "caller" in the middle. Some ideas for images are: Charlie's Angels, Elephant, Egg Salad Sandwich, Palm Tree, Choir, Trap Door, Helicopter, Rolls Royce, and Donkey—see illustration!

6-10 minutes.

Charlie's Angels

Egg Salad Sandwich

Choir

Elephant

Donkey

Helicopter

Palm Tree

Trap Door

Wah

Whole group

One person in the circle claps once, pointing with his hands to someone else in the circle and saying "Wah!" The recipient responds (on the next beat) by raising her arms overhead with her palms together, also saying "Wah!" Finally, the people on either side of the recipient bring their palms together and swing their arms towards the mid-section of the recipient, as if about to "slice" her in half (their arms become like a baseball bat and they are taking a swing towards the recipient without touching her) together in unison, also saying "Wah!" The Wah's are happening on a beat and the rhythm is moderate. So it sounds like "Wah! Wah! Wah!" After the recipient person gets "sliced" by her neighbors, she sends the Wah out to a new person. (Student)

4 minutes.

A What?!

Whole group

The person who starts has two small random objects, such as a roll of scotch tape and a tennis ball. This person passes one of the objects to the person next to her, giving it a gibberish name.

First person to second person: "This is a shmugaloo."
Second person: "A what?"
First person: "A shmugaloo."
Second person takes the object and says to third person: "This is a shmugaloo."
Third person to second person: "A what?"
Second person to first person again: "A what?"
First person repeats to second person: "A shmugaloo."

Second person to third person: "A shmugaloo."
The third person now takes the object from the second person and begins the process with the next person. In this fashion "A what?" and then confirmation of the object's name ("a shmugaloo") is passed back to the initial person every time before object changes hands, until it finally goes all the way around the circle back to the person who started.

When the first object has reached the fourth or fifth person, the first person can begin passing the second object around in the same fashion—in the other direction. So the first person now says to the person on his left, "This is a ramadamalama." "A what?" "A ramadamalama," passing the second object. Passing a second object the other way is optional and heats things up a bit. Game is over when object/s return to first person.

10 minutes.

The Embrace

Partners

Partners spread out in the room and begin in an embrace. The facilitator instructs them to close their eyes and turn away from each other. Following the facilitator's count everyone in the room takes seven steps out into space. She then cues them to turn back toward their partner (or where they think their partner is as their eyes are closed!) and, following her count, everyone takes seven steps, hopefully back towards their partners and into their partners' arms. You can also do this same sequence, but instead of starting with a hug, one partner goes down on one knee and with the other leg provides a bench. This partner keeps her eyes open. The other partner, eyes closed, begins seated, perched on his partner's thigh. He then moves out into space, following the facilitator's count, and then tries to find his partner's "bench" again upon his return. Then switch. (Augusto Boal)

5 minutes (both partners).

Jeepers Creepers

Whole group

In a standing circle, people look down at the ground while someone counts 1, 2, 3. On 3 everyone looks up at a specific person in the circle. If that person is looking back (making eye contact) then those two people scream "Die!" and fall to the ground. Whoever has "died" stands back up, and the whole circle begins another round. Generally, you play 4 or 5 rounds. (Lola Broomberg)

2 minutes.

Start/stop verbal

One team at a time

A group of 4-5 actors stand in a line center stage facing the audience. They may have been assigned a topic by the audience—as a group or individually—or each actor decided the topic of his own monologue. At the facilitator's cue, all the actors begin to speak at once, telling their stories directly to the audience. When someone in the line stops speaking, all the actors stop mid-sentence (as if someone has pressed "pause"). When another person begins talking again, the others begin as well. Be sure to differ the lengths of time for speaking and pausing. Also, make sure the actors find and maintain the same volume.

3 minutes each group.

Instinctive Counting

Small groups

I often follow Urban Ball with this game as they resemble each other in form and objective. However where UB is loud and energetic, this game is much quieter and requires a great deal of concentration. The group members sit or stand in a circle (perhaps 7-10 people) and try to count as high as they can together as a group. Anyone can begin. You try to sense if it's "your turn" to speak. If two members say a number at the same time, the group goes back to "one". You cannot say a number twice in a row. The group may want to try the exercise with eyes closed. Don't rush. And breathe! (Heather Robb.)

10 minutes.

Commonalities

Partners, then groups of four

In partners, you try to think of something you have in common that is not visible and possibly even obscure. The facilitator can invite couples to share with the whole group. Then each dyad connects with another dyad, and the four people have to think of something else the four of you have in common (again, not visible and maybe even obscure or not obvious; in other words, dig a little). Groups can be invited to share. The facilitator can then bring groups of four together to make 8 person groups (or ask the groups to separate and make new groups of 6 and repeat the exercise). The task can be challenging with a large group and can take a while to complete.

10 minutes.

I want...

Whole group

The group lies down in a circle with heads towards the middle. The facilitator (who remains outside the circle) offers incomplete sentences, which each person fills in when it is their turn. The first prompt may be: "I want..." and a designated first person in the circle completes the sentence out loud (he does not repeat "I want") by simply saying "candy." The next person follows right away "love," and the next "a vacation," "new clothes," "inner-peace," etc. until the sentence has traveled all the way around the circle. After the last person completes the sentence, the facilitator offers another prompt: "I am afraid of..." and the group members complete this sentence. It is good if people don't hem and haw and think too much about their answer, but just say the first thing that comes into their head. You might offer 7-10 prompts (depending on group size). This exercise has the sound of a collective poem. (Deb Margolin)

Depends on group size; 5-10 minutes.

Association circle

Whole group

This is a free association exercise as well as another modality for creating a group poem. One person in the circle offers a word (one word) to the person on either side of him: Lemon. The next person offers the first word that comes to mind to the next person: Sour. The next person may say Milk after hearing the word "sour," and so on around the circle. The goal is to free associate off the word just offered to you, not a word a few beats before. Another goal is to reach for interesting words, rather than bland or vague terms. So the "poem" may go like this: Dictionary-Grandmother-Lentils-Brown-Mud-Wrestle-Pretzel-Twisted-Demented-Murder-Blood-Wedding-Veil-Hide-Seek-Enlightenment. At some point, after several go-rounds, you may want to end the poem and reverse directions. (Nina Wise)

5-7 minutes.

Endowment circle

Whole group

This exercise teaches about endowment. The facilitator "brings out" (in pantomime) various objects to pass around the circle: a cup of hot chocolate, a very sharp sword, a snowball, a small kitten, etc. As students pass the objects around they need to make holding and passing this object believable to the others watching by paying close attention to weight, temperature, size, dimension, texture, and remain consistent with their choices.

Depends on group size.

Rainstorm

Whole group

This is a great game for an opening activity. Great with young people. The facilitator explains to the group: "Together we are going to create a rainstorm. Just do as I do and pass the gesture around the circle as it comes to you." Gestures sent around the circle by facilitator are, in this order: SLOW SNAPS, CLAPS, SLAP THE THIGHS, THEN SLAP THIGHS WHILE STOMPING THE FLOOR (peak of storm), SLAP THIGHS, CLAPS, SNAPS. Facilitator begins next gesture when one goes all the way around the circle. It is nice to end the game with inviting everyone to make a sunshine gesture/movement.

5 minutes.

Let's sing!

Small groups or partners

A fun and unthreatening way to get people to sing is to have people pair up, or get into small groups, and come up with a short song or chorus/refrain that everyone in the group knows. There is a short period of time for "rehearsal" and then the groups are invited to sing their song to the group. The goal is not necessarily to sound good or sing in tune, but to simply sing together and enjoy ourselves!

10 minutes.

Sheep shepherd

Whole group

Half the group sits in chairs in a circle and the other half of the group members stand behind the chairs. One chair is empty, but there is an actor behind the empty chair. The people sitting are the sheep. The people standing are the shepherds. The objective is to have a sheep in your chair (pasture) at all times. There will always be one sheep short (one empty chair). The way to get a sheep over to your pasture is for a shepherd to call them—verbally or non-verbally. The way shepherds keep their sheep from "running to greener pastures" is to tap (not slap!) the sheep in the shoulder/upper-back region as the actor tries to leave the chair. If you succeed in tapping the sheep before it bolts, it has to stay with you (if tapped on the lower-back region the sheep is free to go). Shepherds will find various strategies to keep or call their sheep and the sheep will find strategies for escape. (Helen White)

8-10 minutes.

Blowing in the wind

Whole group

This is my adaptation of When the Big Wind Blows. Everyone is seated in a circle in chairs except for someone standing in the middle. In this version the person in the middle says something true about himself, e.g., "I am the youngest sibling" or "I am afraid of heights" or "My favorite holiday is Halloween." If the statement is true for anyone else in the circle they need to get up and find a new chair (and cannot go back to the chair they came from). During the scramble, the "teller" is also trying to find a chair. One person will always be out of a chair and then it is this person's turn to share a truth. Big Wind Blows is the same game except the statements are not formed as "I" statements. Instead the person in the middle says, "The big wind blows for anyone with long hair." Or "The big wind blows for anyone who speaks more than one language."

10 minutes.

Yes

Whole group

This game is challenging and requires practice and patience. (You don't bring this one out right away.) To be successful at this game it is important to concentrate and stay calm. One person begins by making eye contact with someone across the circle (not someone next to you). Once the recipient notices that she is being "chosen" she says to the first person "Yes". Once the person who initiated the eye contact receives a "yes" (and only when!) he begins to walk to the recipient's spot. During this time the recipient makes eye contact with someone new across the circle, and only when she receives a "yes" from that person does she begin to walk to that third person's place—she should find a place to go before the first person gets to her spot. It often takes a group a few tries to understand the sequence of things, but once it does the group can find a wonderful rhythm, almost a dance.

Variation (this is also a useful name game): Say "yes" and the person's name. "Yes, Jo" and Jo cannot start walking until she hears her name.

8-10 minutes.

1-20-1

Whole group

This is a rhythm game. The objective is for the group to count up to 20 (on a beat) and then back down to 1. One person is the beat-holder and snaps her fingers to a moderate tempo. She says "1" and passes the turn to someone else in the circle with her eyes and possibly a slight lean forward toward that next person. This person says "2" without missing a beat, and passes the count to a new person (while she says "2") using eye contact and possibly a small lean forward. Eventually someone passes "19" and the next person says/passes "20" and the next person says "19" and the group counts back down to "1" again. The beat is kept throughout. If/when the group "messes up" and misses a beat or gets a number wrong (the 19-20-19 is often a tricky spot), the group begins again at "1." (Student)

10 minutes.

Minute

Whole group

This exercise raises our awareness about time. I know two versions. The first is to have everyone sit down on the floor. Explain that the objective is to stand up when they feel one minute has passed. The facilitator watches the clock and notes who stood up at or around one minute. End the game at 1.5 or 2 minutes. You can repeat the exercise by having the students start standing up and the objective now is to take one full minute to reach the ground. Again the facilitator times the activity and notes who sat down close to or at one minute.

1 minute each version.

Burning question

Whole group

This is a nice game to start a session with or to use with a new group to break the ice and build trust. Each person simply asks the person to his left (or right) a burning question (anything s/he wants to know about this person) in turn so the whole group can hear the answer. The questions might be anything from "What is your favorite thing to eat for dinner?" to "What is your deepest fear?" depending on how well the group members know each other. If a question ever feels too personal, the recipient always has the prerogative to say, "Too personal, another question please."

10 minutes.

Yes, let's!

Whole group

The mantra of this game is "Yes, let's!" which I will have the group rehearse a few times before we start to get everyone in the mood. I often designate a place in the room from where the offers are made. From this spot, someone offers the group a suggestion (or in improv terms, an "offer"), such as "Let's pretend that we are aliens from outer space arriving on planet earth for the first time!" The group, in unison, responds "Yes, let's!" and then immediately acts out the suggestion, all becoming each person's own version of an extra-terrestrial being exploring planet earth. (Suggestions can be simple actions as well, like "Let's all touch the window!" or "Let's all jump up and down!")

After a minute or two, someone else goes to the "suggestion" spot. When the group sees someone in that spot, everyone stops the action and freezes, waiting to hear the next suggestion: "Let's pretend that we are melting ice cream cones on a hot summer day!" to which the group responds "Yes, let's!" and becomes melting ice cream cones. Ideally, everyone in the group has a turn (depending on the group's size) and people are mindful of not going twice until everyone who wants to has had a turn. After we have played for a while, I often go to the spot and say "Let's end this game!"

Variation: You can also set this game up in partners. One partner suggests an activity, both parties exclaim "Yes, let's!" and begin the activity until the other partner suggests something different. Sometimes I begin in partners and move into the whole group version.

10 minutes (whole group version).

Synchrotalk

Partners

Partners stand facing one another, about one foot apart.
Partner A begins to speak freely about his/her day
or week, as if answering the question "How are you?"
Partner B tries to follow Partner A's dialogue by saying
the exact same words at the same time as they escape
from A's mouth, as if Partner B has crawled inside A's
head—speaking in unison. B tries to fall into the rhythm
and cadence of A's speech by landing directly on top of
as many words as possible, rather than being an echo.
Switch roles.

5 minutes.

What are you lookin' at?

Small groups

Each team (5-8 people) decides on a "spectacle" that
they are watching (e.g., a tennis match, or a pogo stick
contest, or a magician doing tricks). Then they stand
or sit on stage, usually in a line or clump, and simply
imagine they are watching this event. There is no talking
in this exercise and minimal movement, but the reaction
(which can be subtle) is so authentic and honest that
the audience often can guess what it is that they are
watching. The trick is to "keep it real" and not fall into
indicating or overreacting. (Spolin adaptation)

10 minutes.

Shadow walk

Partners

This could also be called follow the leader. Partner A,

who is in front, leads B around the room, expressing herself freely physically and vocally. The journey can take the partners onto the floor, up into the air, etc. It is a stream of consciousness exercise using one's body and voice. B follows A's sound and movement as best s/he can, acting as A's "shadow". Switch roles when facilitator calls time.

6 minutes (3 minutes each).

Mirrors

Partners

This is a classic acting exercise, one that probably needs little explanation. Two people stand a few feet apart. One person begins to initiate movement slowly with some part of his body (hands, head, bending his knees, facial expression); the other person, as his mirror image, follows the movement with her body. The key is to move very slowly, like tai chi, and to maintain eye contact, so that both people will be using their peripheral vision. An audience member should not be able to tell who the leader is. At some point the facilitator cues the partners to switch leaders, and without stopping the movement, the other person begins to initiate. After this person has had equal time, the cue to switch may happen more rapidly and the initiation of the movement and rotation of the leadership should be seamless.

10 minutes.

River

Whole group

This exercise can be done in the round or with a stage area and an audience. One actor begins and strikes a still, silent image (pose) with his body. A second actor strikes a second still, silent image in relation to the first. A third actor strikes a final image building on the "story" or composition that is emerging. After a beat, the first actor exits the stage, leaving the second and third actors in their original positions. Immediately the story changes. A new actor joins offering a new image to complete the set. The actor in the longest exits after a beat. In this way, there is a constant stream or river of images, constantly taking on new shapes and contours and meaning. (Viewpoint adaptation)

5-7 minutes.

Zoomy Zoomy

Whole group

I discovered this game in Prospect Park when I came across a bunch of teenage girls playing and they asked if I wanted to join in. One person starts off as "Zoomy Zoomy" and then the group counts off from 1 to her left. (Zoomy Zoomy, 1, 2, 3, 4, 5, etc.). ZZ sets a tempo using her hands with a clap/clap, thigh/thigh, clap/clap, thigh/thigh; everyone joins in. (If it is a big group, you may want to do snaps instead of claps for volume control.) ZZ starts by saying "Zoomy Zoomy, three three," (or any other number) coordinating her words with the claps and thigh slaps. 3 picks it up right away and says, "Three three, seven seven." On the very next beat, 7 responds, "Seven seven, Zoomy Zoomy. (You can pick any other number, or Zoomy Zoomy.) The game continues (always staying on the rhythm): "Zoomy Zoomy, six six", "Six six, two two" and so on. If anyone misses a beat or messes up a number, he becomes Zoomy Zoomy and the previous ZZ takes his number. To clarify: you say your number first (twice) and then someone else's (twice).

8-10 minutes.

Sound jam

Whole group

Someone starts a vocal "riff," ideally something repeatable and with a down beat. The person to his left or right adds on her own sound/song, blending her voice with his. The next person adds in. And so on until the whole circle has created a sound jam (hopefully, to a common tempo), much like a jazz band with a variety of instruments and vocalists. Once the circle moves around to the first person again, he drops out, and then the second person, and the third, sounds falling away until only the last person's sound is left—and she finds a way to end the song.

Variation: One person starts, the next person in the circle joins in, then the next, until there are four. Each adds to the sounds that the others are making, building on their rhythms and harmonies. Then the first person drops out, so now there are three people singing. After a few seconds the fifth person in the circle joins in, so now there are four again. Then the second person drops out, and so on. Once it gets going there are always between three and four people singing.

Depends on group size; generally 10 minutes.

2 up, 1 down

Whole group

This is an energetic ensemble-building warm up. The group stands in two lines facing each other about 6-8 feet apart. The objective for the whole group is to always

have 3 people in the middle, two "up" and one "down".
Again, it is up to the whole ensemble to maintain this
configuration. Three begin to move around in the middle,
two of them stay vertical on their feet, and the third
dances low down, making sure his/her tail stays near to
the ground. Who is up and who is down is fluid and is
constantly changing: the person down can come up and
then it is up to one of the other two (vertical) dancers to
go down.

In addition, people from the outside can enter the
dance at any time, which would force one (two, three) of
the dancers in the middle back out to the line. The three
movers in the middle stay in constant motion and the
identity of the three keeps changing, as do their levels.
If, for instance, one of the middle three is getting tired
and needs a break, she can step into the "sideline" on
either side, but that means someone has to jump in to
complete the sum of three. If you really get cooking, you
can increase the middle number to five movers at a time,
three up and two down. (Viewpoints)

10 minutes.

Jump at the same time

Whole group

Standing in a circle, the goal is for everybody to jump at
the same time. As this is easier said than done, it requires
patience and several attempts. Once you achieve a true
group jump (with no obvious initiators) then you can try
for two or three in a row. (Viewpoints)

5 minutes.

Explosion

Whole group

Stand in a big circle. The object here is to simultaneously run together into the center of the circle. Again, there should be no individual initiators or leaders. (Viewpoints)

5 minutes.

Glass cobra

Whole group

This is a blind trust-building exercise. In a circle, everyone turns a quarter turn so that they are all looking at the back of someone's head. (The circle has now become a snake, with the head and tail connected.) Everyone closes their eyes and are given 15 seconds or so to "take in" the details of the person in front of them—with their tactile sense—by touching the back of their heads, their backs, etc. with their hands. Then the facilitator says "World!" and the snake parts move out into space, exploring the "world" with the other senses and without sight.

After 4 or 5 minutes the facilitator says "Snake!" and people start to move back to where they feel the center of the room is. The objective is to find (without opening your eyes) the same person you were standing behind before you left. Once you find this person you hold on to his shoulders. The game is over when the Cobra has reassembled itself in the original formation and all its parts are connected again. Then and only then do people open their eyes. It is good to debrief this exercise. (Augusto Boal, as taught to me by Marc Weinblatt)

10 minutes.

Heather 5/6

Whole group, two lines

The group stands in two lines facing each other a couple of feet apart. One line is the 5-count line and the other is the 6-count line. Both lines take a step toward each other, clap, and say "One!" all together. Both lines then turn on "2" and walk away from each other, counting each step. The whole group keeps the same rhythm. The 5-count line takes five steps, counting as they go, then starting the count again: "One! Two! Three! Four! Five! One!" etc. When they get to "One!" they clap, then turn back on "Two!" and walk back towards center. They keep doing this—stepping forward and clapping on "One," then turning on "Two." Meanwhile, the 6-count line does the same thing, but takes six steps instead of five, also clapping and stepping forward on "One" and turning on "Two."

At a certain very exciting point both groups will reunite at the center and have the same "One!" again. Once the groups have the knack, do the exercise with no counting aloud (just clapping on "One"). It can help for the facilitator to keep time with a drum or other percussion instrument (or clapping). (Heather Robb)

10 minutes.

Guess Who?

Whole group

Materials: index cards

Everyone writes down a fact about herself or himself they don't think anyone else in the room knows. The cards are shuffled and then each person picks one (not their own). They have 3 minutes or so in a kind of "market" atmosphere to go around and quiz people, trying to identify the owner of the card they are holding. After a few minutes, everyone gathers in a circle. Each person reads out loud what is written on the card, the group offers a drum roll, and then the reader takes a guess. If wrong, the rightful author gets to reveal himself. (Helen White and Chris Vine)

8 minutes.

1, 2, 3, 4

Solo

One person goes up at a time beginning on stage right. Step 1 is entrance—s/he finds a way to enter the stage purposefully (it could just be to walk on stage). Step 2 is breath: the actor becomes conscious of her/his breath. Step 3 is action—s/he does something—anything. Step 4 is exit—the actor finds a way to exit the stage—again with purpose, confidence, and dignity. The facilitator can assign more specific instructions for each step, e.g., a certain way to enter and/or exit. The action could be singing a measure of a song or share something from your life—or leave it wide open.

Depends on group size.

Car/driver

Partners

In pairs, one person stands behind the other with her hands on his shoulders. The front person is the "car," the back person is the "driver." The front person closes his eyes, and at the cue of the facilitator, all the drivers begin to take their car out "for a drive" moving carefully through the space. It is good to remind everyone that this is a trust exercise and the most important goal is to keep your car safe. I usually add, "No nicks, scratches, dents or bumps!" Each driver will be able to sense how comfortable their car is moving blindly and can determine what speed is appropriate. After a little while, I invite the drivers to choose a "destination spot" in the room and steer their car to that spot. Once they arrive, they squeeze the car-person's shoulders and the cars open their eyes—in front of them will be an image chosen by the driver: a window, a red curtain, someone else's face. Then you switch roles. Discussion is important for this exercise, either in between or after (in partners and then with whole group), as it often raises varying levels of fear and/or discomfort for some people.

10 minutes.

Carpool

Partners

This next step in Car/driver I learned from my dad. I've named it Carpool. After the drivers are out "driving" with their cars, at the facilitator's cue "Carpool!" the drivers carefully, gracefully begin to pass the cars around. While moving through space, two drivers make eye contact and seamlessly swap cars—never leaving a car to run on its own—there always is a hand on his/her shoulder. The swapping continues until the facilitator instructs everyone to retrieve their own car back, find a destination, squeeze shoulders, open eyes. (Jonathan Fox)

5 minutes.

Hit the shoe

One person at a time

A shoe is placed in the middle of the room. You want to have an open space for this exercise. The actors line up at the edge of the space with blindfolds (if you have them) or prepared to close their eyes. Each actor takes a turn walking blindly but purposefully through space with the goal of hitting the "mark" (the shoe). The actor walks and stops when she feels she has reached the shoe, she bends down and deliberately puts her hand down on the shoe (or not). Only after she has reached for the shoe does she open her eyes to see if she was close or not. Encourage your students to walk with purpose, confidence and conviction- and to trust their intuition! You return to the back of the line after taking a turn. Generally, everyone has 3 or 4 tries. (Judith Sloan)

Depends on group size; generally, 10 minutes.

Village

Whole group

On small pieces of paper the facilitator writes down numbers for each person in the group—so if there are 12 people in the group, she numbers pieces of paper 1 to 12 and has each person take one. (It's good to explain to people ahead of time what's going to happen.) Once everyone has a designated number, people begin moving around the room. It is nice to imagine that we all live in the same village and are going about our daily tasks. The facilitator calls out a number. The person whose number is called, cries out, and then "faints" or falls towards the ground. The rest of the villagers rush to his side and catch him as he falls. Even if you are not directly holding the faller, you can support the supporters. In this way the whole village comes out in support when someone falls. The faller is brought back to his feet and he, along with everyone else, goes on about his day, moving about the village. Another number is called and the same sequence occurs: a verbal cue, fall, and catch/recover. This is a trust fall exercise, so it is great to really take a risk when your number is called (and trust that the group will be there to catch you) and very important to rush to the faller when you know who it is to prevent him from reaching the ground. It is equally important for everyone to be prepared to fall all the way to ground safely in the rare cases that that happens. At the end, the facilitator can call more than one number at once to get things really active. (Augusto Boal, as taught to me by Marc Weinblatt. Boal's version is called "Fainting at Frejus.")

10 minutes.

Movement telephone

Teams of 6-8

Actor/dancers stand in a line facing stage right, profile to the audience. The first person (stage right) makes up a short movement phrase (2 counts of 8 or so). He makes sure he can remember and repeat it. When he is ready, he taps the person in front if him, who turns around, and shows her the phrase (only once!). This person then taps the next person, who turns around, and the mover repeats the phrase exactly as she saw it, and the phrase, or "rumor", moves down the line. Whoever is receiving should repeat the phrase exactly, including pauses, "ums," giggling, etc. The final person does the phrase to the audience, who then compares it to the original, which is repeated by the choreographer or first person. You may ask two or three teams to do the exercise in turn. (Francis Batten)

3 minutes for each team.

Bodypart alive

Solo

This is an exercise that raises awareness in different parts of our body and warms a group up to the idea of *embodying* emotions/ideas/inanimate objects (a key component of Playback Theatre acting). The facilitator cuts up small pieces of paper and asks students to write down 1) a body part and 2) a feeling. The pieces of paper (two from each person) are put into two separate hats. Each person, one at a time, picks a piece of paper out of each hat (an emotion and a body part), and then this person "moves" this emotion across the stage with the assigned body part. So the person might be articulating "anger" with her knees or "joy" with his pelvis. You can have people write down ideas instead of emotions.

30 seconds each person.

Metaphors

Partners

Take turns in dyads sharing all or some of the following: If you were a tree, what kind of tree would you be and why? If you were a body of water, what kind of water would you be and why? Book? Album cover? Kind of drink? Kind of music? Hat? Kitchen utensil? Landscape? Word? Obviously you can use these and/or make up your own. (Inspired by Peter Hall)

10 minutes.

Essence & metaphor

Partners or small groups

This exercise offers an opportunity to practice getting at the heart of the story as well as to train the brain to think metaphorically. In small groups someone tells a short story from his/her life (for about 3-4 minutes). Then another person in the group comes up with the heart or essence of the story as s/he heard it. Another person in the group suggests a metaphor for the story. A fourth person (if there is one) could next suggest an idea of how the metaphor could be translated in sound/movement/text on stage. Finally, the original teller reflects back whether the suggested essence of the story and metaphor resonates.

Each person may have a turn telling a story or just a couple of people, depending on group size and time constraints.

6-8 minutes each person.

Two truths and a lie

Whole group or small groups

Each person thinks up two truths and a lie about her/his life and shares this with the group. The group has to determine which of the three pieces of information is not true. The information can be facts or small stories/experiences. Best to do this in groups no bigger than 10 people.

10 minutes.

Battleship

Partners

Need blindfolds

People are in teams of two. One person is blindfolded—this person is both the "target" and the "firing squad". The other person is the communicator, or "control tower". Each team of two gets a paper ball (crunched up piece of paper), which is handled by only the blindfolded member. The goal is to get as many "hits" as you can. You score when the blindfolded person throws a paper ball and hits another blindfolded person. The communicator directs the blindfolded team member with her/his voice only (no touching). This is a hilarious game to watch—it's fun to break the group into two and create an audience while 3 or 4 teams play on stage—and then switch. (Inspired by Maddy Fox)

10 minutes.

Minis

Partners

In dyads, partner A shares a short current story from her/his life (the facilitator may have offered a theme). Often I time these (3-4 minutes) so that everyone starts and ends at the same time. Partner B listens attentively. When the time is up for the storytelling, B stands up and plays back the story she heard in three moments (beginning, middle, and end of story, or the story's main three essences) in frozen, silent pictures. The actor holds each image for a beat and then moves to the next. If done well, A will see his story, or at least the essence of it.

5 minutes.

Change 3 things

Partners

With partners standing facing each other, the facilitator gives everyone 30--60 seconds to have a good look at each other. Then, either at the same time, or one at a time, you turn away from each other and change three things about your physical appearance (pull your shirt out if it was tucked in, or roll up your pants, or put a bracelet on the other wrist, or take your glasses off, and so on). After you have adjusted 3 things, the facilitator cues everyone to turn back around to face their partners and each person has to try to guess what has been changed. Then switch.

5 minutes.

Turn around

Group

The facilitator asks half the group to come onto stage and stand in a line facing upstage. She has prepared a list of questions for the group on stage to "answer". The actors on stage simply turn around and face the audience for a beat when the answer is "me" and then turn back upstage and wait for the next question. The questions are tailored to the age and demographic of the group and might be designed around a theme. They might include: Who is the oldest sibling in their family? Who likes chocolate ice cream? Who likes to fly in a plane? Who was born in another country? And, eventually, Who has ever lied to a loved one? Who has had someone close to them die? Who believes in capital punishment? This exercise works especially well with young people. Be sure to think carefully about what questions you ask and why!

8-10 minutes.

Two by three by Bradford

Partners

Partners stand 2-3 feet apart facing each other. They begin to count "1, 2, 3" together:

A: 1

B: 2

A: 3

B: 1

A: 2

B: 3

The goal is to count together as smoothly and seamlessly, and with as much speed, as possible. Next, one of the partners in each team is instructed to replace number "1" with a random sound and movement (such as jumping in the air and saying "meow"), which now both parties do from now on instead of saying "1." So the dialogue becomes "Meow, 2, 3, meow, 2, 3." Next the other partner replaces number 2 with a brand new sound and movement (such as flicking the hips and saying "whoosh"). So the dance now goes, "Meow, whoosh, 3, meow, whoosh, 3." Finally, you get rid of numbers entirely and the partner who created a S & M for number 1, makes a final S & M for number 3, so the final dialogue/dance might go: "Meow, whoosh, tada!, Meow, whoosh, tada!" I often go around the room and let each couple do their dance in front of the other groups for a few seconds as they are very entertaining. (Augusto Boal)

10 minutes.

Mapping/
Sociometry

Sociometry (from Psychodrama) is a way to make visible some of the underlying connections, differences, and relationships in a group through a kind of physical mapping. When skillfully done it helps to include people who might otherwise be on the margins for any reason. Sociometry is commonly used in Playback workshops and it is an effective tool for building trust and community within any group.

Spectrums

Whole group

Typically near the beginning of every Playback workshop there is a sociometry or mapping section at which time people are asked to place themselves on a spectrum illustrating how much Playback experience they are coming in with. "Line up on this end of the spectrum if you have no experience, and on the other end if you have many years of experience." People place themselves on the spectrum wherever they feel is appropriate—they may need to chat to each other to decide where they fit. Then people are invited to speak from their place if they wish. Other typical spectrum questions are "Line up according to how nervous you feel right now" or "Line up according to how comfortable you are performing on stage," etc. It is good if the lines curve in a half circle so that everyone can see each other.

7 minutes per spectrum.

Where did you come from?

Whole group

Ask participants to create a geographical map using the whole room, showing the place in the world that they traveled from to come to the workshop—thus literally creating a map with their bodies. Especially with an international group, this is a good opportunity to bring out concerns such as language.

7-10 minutes

Who do you know?

Whole group

Ask participants to place a hand on the shoulder of anyone they knew before the workshop began. This shows right away already established connections that might exist in the group (company members, spouses, roommates, and so on).

5 minutes.

Standing together

Whole group/small groups

If it is a Playback workshop, the facilitator may want to ask any Playback Theatre company members to stand with each other (and/or company directors, Playback teachers, etc.).

5 minutes.

Cross the room

Two groups

This can be done with a facilitator reading out prompts and/or the participants making up their own categories. It is nice to combine the two. There are two groups standing 20 feet apart or so. (Or you can start as one group on one side of the room and pretty soon there will be two groups facing each other.) The facilitator will say, "Cross the room if..." then name a category.

The questions should be relevant to the demographic of the group as well as any theme you might be exploring. Whoever feels they are part of that category crosses over to the other side. After people have crossed, another prompt is given. Some possible prompts: Cross the room if... you will be graduating soon; are the oldest sibling; are the baby of the family; are somewhere in between; were born in another country; speak another language; like school; find school challenging; feel optimistic about your future; have gotten in trouble lately; are in love. And then you can encourage the group to move deeper: if your parents are divorced; if you grew up below poverty level; if there was abuse in your family; if you struggle with addiction; if you are afraid of being alone, etc. Next, you invite a volunteer to come to the head of the two lines on either side and offer a category of his/her own. Then offer this opportunity to others. It is important to debrief this exercise—either as a whole group or in small groups.

10 minutes.

Clumping

Whole group

Ask the group to cluster up in the middle of the room. Tell them that we are going to get to know one another a bit as well as find out what we have in common. Invite someone to peel away from the clump, walk to another place in the room and share something about herself (I love dark chocolate; I love to skydive; I am a grandfather; I am a cancer survivor; I am bisexual; I struggle to tell people how I truly feel; I am a single parent). If this statement is true for anyone else they walk and join the person who spoke, creating a new clump. (But if they prefer not to reveal this information about themselves, they don't have to.) Someone else peels away (from either clump), walks to a new place, and shares a truth. If there are others who resonate with what has been said, they join this person, creating a third clump. And so on. It is good to stress that there is no conversation, discussion or judgment about what has been shared.

10 minutes.

Identity circle

Whole group

This exercise offers people a chance to explore the complexity of identity, especially how one's social identity can become a target of systematic oppression or alienate someone from a dominant group. It's important to explain ahead of time that we're looking for aspects of social identity—gender, age, sexual orientation, religion, race, class, etc—not personality (unlike in the "Clumping" exercise). (The facilitator will probably need to precede the exercise with some discussion about the ways human beings are different from each other, and invite participants to think about their identity in this way.) This exercise can go quite deep and often requires some kind of whole or small group (or Playback) debriefing afterwards.

People stand in a circle. When someone feels moved to speak, he takes one step into the circle and says, "I am African-American." Anyone else in the circle who identifies with the statement also takes a step in, joining the speaker in solidarity for a moment. Then everyone, including the person who spoke, steps back into the main circle. When she is ready another person will step in, "I am a woman." Anyone else who identifies as a woman steps in. And so on. There is no talking or dialogue except for the first person who steps in naming an identity.

Other identities that may be raised are: I am Jewish; I am Muslim; I am Latina; I was raised by a single parent; I grew up poor; I am gay. The facilitator should explain that no one has to "out" herself or himself unless they want to.

10 to 15 minutes.

Main

Activities

Main activities are, for one reason or another, weightier than the warm-up activities. Many of the following exercises can certainly be used as warm-up, but also can stand as the "main lesson" of the session. Some Playback Theatre short forms are included in this section as they take time to learn and offer a space for personal stories to be told.

Machines

Teams

This is the classic acting "machine" with an added part. Teams of 4 or 5 actors stand upstage in neutral. One person steps out center stage and does a repetitive (even rhythmic) sound and movement. Once the first person's sound and gesture is established, the second actor steps out offering a different sound and movement, physically connected to the first, and then the third, and fourth. Each actor should offer something different to have as many textures and layers to the machine as possible, fitting in, however, to the rhythm and aesthetic of what has already been established. It is important to maintain physical connection and to explore different levels. When the first person out is aware (using her audio sense and peripheral vision) that all the actors are contributing to the machine, she stops her sound and movement, which cues the rest of the actors to stop.

10 minutes.

Landscapes

Small teams

This exercise follows the exact same steps as the familiar "machine" only the actors are embodying certain landscapes volunteered by audience members; therefore the "machine" becomes less robotic, more organic. An audience member might suggest "Caribbean island" or "outer space" or "New York City," and the team of actors creates a moving sculpture depicting this landscape following the same steps as listed above. Pay attention again to creating different levels and textures.

5 minutes.

Fluid sculptures

Teams

Fluid Sculptures are dancing tableaux that represent a feeling or a moment someone has had recently. They are one of the basic performance forms in Playback Theatre. After the moment or feeling is shared from an audience member, the actors step out one at a time to the center of the stage with a repetitive sound and movement, each reflecting an aspect of the teller's experience. After a beat or two, the next actor joins the first, connecting physically as one would in a three dimensional sculpture (as in the machines), adding a different sound and movement (a different texture) and embodying another aspect to the feeling or experience. This action continues until all the actors on stage are contributing to the sounding, moving sculpture. Once the last actor has joined, the sculpture continues moving for another couple of beats and then ends by all the actors stopping together and then acknowledging the teller with a glance. Fluid Sculptures sometimes contain text as well as sounds. (Playback Theatre)

3 minutes per sculpture.

Pairs

Partners

Pairs is another basic Playback Theatre performance form. It offers us the opportunity to reflect on a situation or relationship in life which is pulling us in opposite directions at the same time, such as love and hate, excitement and nervousness, resentment and gratitude, eagerness and hesitation. Actors pair up on center stage, one standing behind the other, both facing the audience. Typically there are two or three sets of pairs, or 4-6 actors lined up in twos. After an audience member has shared her pair of conflicting emotions, the pair positioned on stage right begins the action. Without speaking or any preparation, generally, the front actor begins with movement and non-repetitive sound/words representing *one* of the teller's feelings. Once the second actor is clear on which emotion is being depicted, he embodies the other. Pairs are expressive and physical; however, for the most part, the actors remain stationary, i.e. both actors continue to face front and do not travel the stage. The actors should work to create a gestalt—as both these emotions supposedly co-exist in the teller's psyche—by connecting physically and possibly thematically in their words or sounds. After the first pair is performed, the first actors bring their bodies back to neutral (or freeze in an image), and the next two actors begin their own version of the same internal struggle. Then the final team shows a third depiction. After each pair has performed, the whole ensemble acknowledges the teller with a glance. Ideally, there is contrast between each pair of actors. (Playback Theatre)

1 minute each pair.

Three part story

Groups of three

Three part story is another Playback Theatre short form. Three actors stand upstage in a line, in neutral. After a short life story has been told by someone in the audience, the first actor (stage right) steps forward into the playing space and, using the whole stage, embodies the first sentence or an element of the story, not necessarily chronological, using words, sound, dance, song, poetry, mime—whatever mode of expression the actor chooses. After thirty seconds or so, the first actor freezes in an image and the second actor enters the stage acting out the second part of the story, again using whatever medium he is inspired to use and playing from the perspective of any character in the story. The second actor freezes in an image, possibly in relation to the first actor's image (who has remained frozen) and the third actor comes forward, picking up wherever the second actor left off and embodies the final part of the story. The final moment is a stage picture made by the three actors in their respective frozen shapes.

Although an actor may use the other actors as props or characters to interact with, the actors do not react to one another once they are frozen. The acting in TPS is *abstract*, not literal, and involves movement and metaphor. (Playback Theatre)

5 minutes.

Three sentence story

Groups of three

This form, also a Playback performance form, is similar to Three part story. Invite someone to tell a story in only three sentences, which the facilitator repeats. (The facilitator may need to ask a few questions before repeating the sentences, such as "And how did you feel?" to flesh out the emotional landscape). The first actor embodies the first sentence and freezes, the second actor the second sentence, and the third actor the third sentence.

3 minutes.

Haiku

Groups of three

This is a variation of three sentence story, inspired by Japanese Haiku poetry (though it doesn't attempt the sophistication and subtlety of that long tradition). The facilitator hands out index cards and asks the group members to write a three-line anonymous poem about their lives. (If you like, you can limit the first and third lines to five syllables and the second line to seven syllables.) The cards are put in a hat and shuffled. Someone pulls a poem from the hat and reads it out loud—twice. Then the actors embody the poem following the pattern of three sentence story above. It is nice to rotate poetry readers, actors, and musician in a round-robin format.

Five minutes for writing; three minutes per enactment.

Chorus

Groups of 3 to 5

The Playback chorus was created in Australia by British practitioner Francis Batten, and is inspired by the Greek Chorus. It is used either as a way to playback someone's life story, as an alternative to the Playback *Story (*or *Scene)* (instead of choosing actors and assigning characters) or as a mood sculpture in the background of a story that has been cast and is being acted out. In a full-story chorus three to seven actors begin by standing in a clump upstage center. They breathe together and then one actor offers a sound and movement that the rest of the group follows. Another actor offers the next gesture, based on another element in the story (not necessarily chronological), and then another. The gestures illustrate the various dynamics and plot points of the story. The chorus is enacted as a series of *unison* sound/text and movement gestures offered by the members of the acting team. Unlike a fluid sculpture or a pair, a chorus has the freedom to travel all over the stage. It is important for the actors to synchronize their movements, create contrast between the gestures, and, to rotate who is leading and following. (Playback Theatre)

5 minutes.

3 pictures

Small groups

Actors in small groups think of a story—a fairytale, a historical or current event—that most people in the room would be familiar with. They decide the beginning, middle and end of the story, or three essential moments (what's happening, who are the characters, the emotional landscape, etc, in each moment). Then they stage these moments in three still, silent stage pictures. The group practices moving through the three pictures, remembering what character each person played in which picture (all actors do not have to be in every image). After 5-10 minutes of rehearsal, each group performs its story for the other groups creating the first frozen image, holding for a beat, moving on to the second, and then the third. The audience tries to guess what story is being depicted. It is fun to use fabric or props if they are available and a percussion instrument (played by the facilitator) to accent each picture.

10-12 minutes for the whole group.

Movement/sound/text

Groups of 3

Someone in the audience tells a short personal story. The actors are standing upstage in a line, in neutral. After the story is told, the first actor comes out into the space and does a short piece of improvisational movement (30 seconds). When this actor is finished, she steps back into the line. The second actor takes a step out and creates a short soundscape, responding to the movement. The sounder steps back into the line when he is done. Finally, the third actor steps out (staying in his channel) and offers an improvised piece of text/dialogue/poetry inspired by the movement and sound and original story.

Variation: You can also do this exercise without a personal story as the impetus. Instead, the mover would create the source material.

5 minutes per small group.

Flock

Teams of four

Four actors stand in an open diamond shape, all facing the audience. The person furthest downstage starts out as the "lead bird". The lead bird begins to move downstage finding a repetitive sound and movement; the other actors mimic the lead bird's sound and movement, also moving forward. At some point the lead bird turns in another direction (stage right, left or upstage) and suddenly there is a new lead bird who immediately picks up the dance by changing the step and moving this new sound and movement forward. When she turns, whoever is now in front becomes the new lead bird. The goal is to keep the movement lively and diverse and for the dancers to follow each other like one flock. At some point the facilitator asks the group to "find an ending." This is a great warm up exercise for the Playback Chorus form.

4-5 minutes each flock.

Better to hear you with!

Teams of three.

Three actors stand center stage facing the audience. The center person is the Ear and the people on either side are the storytellers. Either the storytellers choose their own story or a topic or first line is assigned to them by the audience. At the facilitator's cue, the storytellers begin their stories simultaneously, speaking to the center person at the same volume level. The task for the person in the middle is to try to catch as many details from both stories as possible. After a minute or two, the storytellers are cued to stop, and the Ear person reports back to the audience what the two stories were about. "Max was talking about a three-headed monster who kidnapped the school principal."

4 minutes each group.

First line, last line

Teams of two

Two actors go up stage to improvise a scene. The audience gives them a first line and a last line with which to end the scene. The two lines should not be related (e.g., "What is that strange thing in the sky?" "Fried eggs are much better in the evening"). One line is assigned to one actor and the other to the second actor. The scene must begin and end with the assigned lines and nothing before or afterwards (although gesture and movement is okay.) The audience can also supply the actors with their relationship and their whereabouts. The objective is for the actors to create a logical scene that connects the first line to the second while remaining true to their relationship and environment.

Variation: You can also play this with just providing the last line. The line has to lend itself to all kinds of scenarios, such as "I can't believe this is happening!" or "What are we supposed to do now?" Often small scene groups are created and assigned the same last line. They are given time to rehearse and then show their improvised scene for the group—all ending in the same line.

5 minutes each scene.

Podiums

Teams of two

Two people volunteer to be "experts" speaking on two different topics at a conference. The actors stand facing the audience a few feet apart from one another. The audience (or facilitator) gives each "expert" a subject on which s/he will be speaking. Examples might be: Mating Rituals of the Australian Bull Frog and How to Recycle Dirty Socks; or Ancient Cave Drawings of Early Human Activity and The Tibetan Custom for Naming a Child. At the facilitator's cue the two presenters begin their speeches, doing their best to sound knowledgeable on the subject (of course, the goal is to sound confident, i.e.

it is more important how you say it, not what you say). When possible the two experts, who are speaking at the same time, start to "steal" words or phrases from each other speeches, incorporating overheard words into their own speech as best they can. The idea is to repeat and use the word right away. So you are continuing with your own "talk" but gracefully adopting words from the other expert's speech.

5 minutes each team.

Standing ovation

Group with one solo at a time

Someone volunteers to go out of the room. The rest of the group decides on a physical task for this person to perform when s/he comes back in. This task should be interactive with the environment, i.e. the features of the room. So the task might be to sit on a particular chair, or open up a particular window, or get under a table, write your name on the chalkboard, or turn off the light. When the group is more experienced with the game, you can suggest compound tasks, such as: put on the hat and stand on the chair, or move the vase of flowers from the bookshelf to the table. The group agrees on the task when the person is out of earshot and then has to communicate this task to the person with clapping only. More clapping means "hot" and less clapping, or no clapping, means "cold". The main tip with this game is to keep the faith! The person will receive the transmission from the group if both parties have patience and the clappers stay focused. When the person successfully completes the task the group stands up and gives this person a standing ovation! (Judith Sloan: renamed here)

5 minutes each person.

Cat in the Hat

Teams of four

Actors assume a diamond formation. One person is the Cat in the Hat and everyone is oriented toward him. The Cat mirrors the person opposite, who begins a movement which the Cat needs to follow (any movement is good—slow, fast, up, down, arms, legs, etc). Next, the person to the Cat's left begins to ask him simple math questions—which the Cat has to answer. Finally, the person to his right begins to ask him personal questions (e.g., How many siblings do you have? What do you eat for breakfast? What is a dream you have for your future?)—which the Cat has to answer while he is mimicking the person opposite and answering the math questions. The Cat tries to stay calm and collected while doing all of these activities simultaneously! (Lola Broomberg, renamed here)

15 minutes.

Food chain

Solo

The actor on stage thinks of a food she either loves or despises. She then begins to walk across the stage as this food (personifying this inanimate object as if it were a character) finding its walk, tempo, facial expression, and sound—embodying this fruit, vegetable, entrée, snack, or dessert. When the actor gets to the center of the stage she turns to the audience and says something in character, finding an appropriate voice but not describing oneself physically. If I was a carrot, for example, I would try to imagine and express "carrot" qualities – "Hi. Hi. How're you feeling today? Want to jog 13 miles?!?"--rather than, "Hi. I am long and orange." After a few words to the audience in character, the actor proceeds moving across to stage left, moving (on her feet) and sounding in the character of this food. Once she has reached the other side of the stage, the audience tries to guess what she was. To make it easier, although it is not necessary, the actor, before or afterward, can stipulate what category her food falls into.

10-12 minutes.

Beat poet

Teams of two

For this exercise you will need a beret (or flamboyant hat) or two, a pair of sunglasses or two, and a drum. Each actor takes a turn at being a "beat poet" (reminiscent of the 1960s Soho beat poets) donning the beret and sunglasses and making up the worst poem imaginable on the spot. It need not make sense in the least but it is physical and dramatic and often an embodied piece of free association. A "musician" accompanies on the drums offering "beats" to the poem. The poems often resemble pieces of performance art. This is a liberating exercise for most people because you cannot do it wrong. There is absolutely no pressure in having to create a "good" poem. Just put on the sunglasses and follow your imagination. (Robin Aronson)

10-15 minutes.

Turning points

Teams of five or six

Five or six actors stand facing upstage. One actor turns to the audience and begins to speak on any subject from a personal point of view ("I")—or to tell a story from her life. When another actor has the impulse, he too swivels around to face the audience and begins to speak—either on another subject or on something related to the first person's account—essentially interrupting the first person. As soon as the second person begins to speak (which should be very soon) the first person swivels back around to face upstage. The second person speaks/recounts until another person interrupts him, at which time this second storyteller turns back around. There is only one person facing the audience and speaking at a time. The turns should be sharp. If an actor didn't reach the "heart" or point of her story, she can turn around again and continue with her original story—or start a new one. The actors continue in this fashion, swiveling back and forth, interrupting each other, telling stories. Often it is a game of free association. The game can be framed, or prompted, by a theme (such as "going to the dentist" or "molasses" or "eyebrows") or be open-ended.

10 minutes.

Arm monologue

Two at a time

One actor stands behind the other, sticking his hands under the front actor's arms, while the front actor wraps his arms behind his back, trying to take his arms out of sight. You are trying to create the illusion that the back actor is not there and his arms and hands belong to the front actor. (Covering the back person with a jacket or sweatshirt can help.) The front person begins a monologue on a topic offered by the audience while the back person gesticulates along with the speech. You can have a few teams of actors go.

3 minutes per team.

Autobiographies

Teams of four

This is my take on a Ruth Zaporah exercise. Four actors sit on chairs facing the audience. One of them begins telling a story—either something spontaneous from his/her life, or inspired by a theme/word someone in the audience throws out. Often I suggest the actors begin with stories from their childhood. One person begins to spontaneously tell his story. When another person in the line is inspired, she interrupts his story and begins to tell hers. She may have been inspired by something he said, from which she free-associates, or she may begin something totally new.

At some point in her story (beginning, end, middle) another person interrupts and begins to speak (it may even be the first teller who resumes telling his initial story). The actors continue their storytelling, interrupting each other at strategic moments, weaving a tapestry of their lives. It is important to note that the actors only interact with the audience, not with each other—they don't look at each other or make third person references to each other's stories, such as "Like he said, I don't like snakes either." Each storyteller is seemingly in her own bubble, or on her own soundtrack. When she is interrupted, she stops immediately, mid-sentence, even mid-word. In this way, there is always only one person speaking at a time.

After a few rounds of seated stories, the actors begin to stand up when they tell their stories. Once all actors are standing, an actor walks downstage with his story. The other actors follow suit, in turn, when they are speaking. Finally, all the actors are standing in a line downstage. Each finds his/her exit line, delivers it and leaves the stage. (Inspired by Ruth Zaporah)

10-15 minutes.

Object exercise

Solo

Each person is asked to bring in an object that has
personal value to him/her (represents family history, or is
a found object, or could be based on whatever theme you
might be exploring). First step is to present the objects to
the rest of the group by telling a story about the object,
explaining why it is important. Next, each actor writes
a monologue (or makes a dance) based on the story
connected to the object or inspired by the object in some
way.

Depends on group size.

Columbian hypnosis

Partners

This is both a great physical warm up as well as an
effective tool to explore issues of power. One partner
stands with her hand 6 inches away from her partner's
face (bottom of hand corresponding with bottom of
chin). This person is the "leader" or the "hypnotist".
When cued by the instructor the leaders begin to move
their partners around the room by moving their hand-
which the followers have to follow intently—never
allowing their face to stray more then 6 inches away and
maintaining the same orientation at all times (eyebrows
to finger tips, base of hand to chin). The leader can move
slow or fast, move around the room or even onto the
floor. This game is fun but it is also about manipulation
and control and almost always people have comments

afterwards. You can debrief after each round, or change roles and then debrief—as partners and with the whole group. (Augusto Boal)

5 minutes each round.

Sad/mad/count

Half the group at a time

This game helps teaches authenticity on stage and supports the Stanislavski principle of emotion from action and not the other way around. Spolin also has a version of this which is more of an orientation exercise. In this version, one half of the group goes up on stage. They are given the simple task to "act sad" (or "scared" or "nervous" or "happy") for one minute. How the actors play this is up to each individual. After one minute the facilitator gives the actors a second task, for example to "act angry" for one minute. Finally, the group is instructed to count something in the workspace, such as lights, or chairs, or panels in the floor. They are all counting the same item. The first person to come up with the right number "wins." This is said simply to create motivation. (Often, I don't even know the correct number of lights myself, as it is irrelevant.) The audience is then asked which of the three "performances" they preferred to watch. Observers will often comment that when actors are engaged in an *action* and genuine activity (and not manufacturing emotion) it is most interesting and engaging. Then the groups switch. (Helen White)

10 minutes total.

Freeze

Whole group

This is a classic improv scene game, either on stage or in a circle. Two actors volunteer to go into the middle. They are given a relationship and a whereabouts (divorcing couple: in a rowboat in the middle of a lake). The actors begin to improvise the scene keeping the scene very physical. There is often dialogue, but it is important that the actors keep moving, with actions appropriate to their given circumstances, as well as keep the scene/plot moving forward. At a certain point, the facilitator (or another actor) yells "Stop!" The actors freeze the action and a third actor steps in, tapping one of the actors (usually the one who has been in longest) and assumes his physical position as closely as possible. Once you are tapped out, you return to the circle, and a brand new scene begins initiated by the person who just came in. It is your physical position that determines the idea for the next scene. The person who taps in starts the scene by giving an offer to the other actor who "accepts" the offer and we have now been transported to a new place with new characters. The divorcees-on-the-lake scene next becomes two penguins looking for food in Antarctica (because something about the physical stance that the new actor took on felt penguin-like). Sometimes it is fun to give everyone in the circle a number and everyone gets a turn to enter when her/his number is up.

10 minutes.

Quick freeze

Two people at a time

This is shorter version of Freeze. One person strikes

a pose in the middle of the circle or up on stage. The pose can be anything. It is a sculpture, an image, that he commits to and holds. Another actor approaches this frozen actor and begins a scene with a line of dialogue, inspired by the image. The first actor unfreezes, accepts the offer/idea, and responds with one line. That is it: a two-line scene, with characters, context, situation. The second actor strikes a new image in the center, holds it, until a third actor approaches and offers a line. I generally cycle through until everyone has gone and we are back to our first actor entering the scene (depending on group size).

10 minutes.

123454321

Up to 5 actors at a time

This is a more advanced form of Freeze. One person begins on stage and is given a who/what/where. (Example: secretly painting a mural on bedroom wall.) She begins the scene, moving the scene forward and keeping it physical. Another actor says "Freeze!" She freezes and he joins her beginning a new two-person scene based on the physical position of the frozen actor. Now it's two toddlers left behind in a department store. At a certain point, a third actor says "Freeze," and joins the two actors, initiating a third scene—a couple at a romantic dinner finds a cockroach on the plate and is telling the waiter. This goes on until there are five actors creating a five-person scene.

Once the fifth actor is in he needs to find a logical reason to exit the scene. If the scene was a basketball game with a bunch of teens, the fifth actor's character-the one who started this scene—realizes he is late for work. As soon as this actor exits the stage, the fourth scene is resumed, and the fourth actor needs to find a logical reason to leave the scene in character. And then it is the third scene, the second, and finally we are back to the initial actor painting her bedroom walls. She finds a way to end the play.

12-15 minutes.

Sit/stand/lie down

3 actors at a time

This is a three-person scene. The physical score is that at all times one actor needs to be sitting, another standing, and the third lying down, all alternating positions throughout the scene. The audience or facilitator gives the actors a who and where and the actors improvise a scene, sticking to the score.

5 minutes each scene.

Emotional memory scenes

Solo

Pen and paper

The facilitator writes a list of emotions, or has them in mind. The emotions I generally use are: fear, strong anger, despair or deep sadness, embarrassment, excitement, true happiness. You ask each participant to recall a memory for each emotion, one at a time. The memories should not be too recent but should still be vivid and elicit a strong emotional response. Actors write down (in a few sentences) any detail they can recall about the experience. No one will be seeing the paper except themselves. You want to prompt people to think of times when they felt these emotions deeply, and give them time to reflect and write before you move to the next one. If someone can't recall a memory, that is fine—they can skip it and/or come back to it later.

When people have recalled an experience for each memory you ask them to note the experience that still feels the strongest—one they would be willing to share with the whole group. Next you invite volunteers to come up to the stage and reenact the experience—just at the peak moment, the reaction to whatever happened, not the incident itself. Ideally, no words are spoken—just the emotional reaction. Generally, I don't have students explain the experience, so the audience may not know exactly what is happening; but the felt sense of the actor is clear.

20 minutes (depending on group size).

Circle story

Whole group or small groups

Either seated or standing up, the group creates a collective story by one person speaking at a time. There are several prompts you can offer. First is that each person contributes one word at a time (including "a" and "the"), together making complete sentences. Ideally, the story has a beginning, middle and goes somewhere. Next, after you've done it one word at a time, you can suggest that people contribute cliff-hanger paragraphs—so each person tells a little piece of the story, perhaps ending their turn in the middle of the sentence—"They came to the bottom of a very large mountain and all of a sudden heard…"—which the next person has to pick up from. Finally, you can use the 1-2-3-4-5 formula. So the first person says one word, the next person adds the next two words, the third person three, etc. After the fifth person contributes five words to the story, the next person either goes back to one word or down to four words. These stories can be theme-based or wide open.

3-5 minutes each story.

Partner story

Partners

This is same game as Circle story, only a story is constructed in pairs facing each other. All of the prompts listed above apply.

3-5 minutes each story.

Choir story

5-10 actors on stage

This is a "circle story" in a line and with someone (the choir conductor) cueing who speaks when. The actors stand in a line with the "conductor" facing them. The conductor points to someone in the line to start the story. When the conductor wants to she points to someone else in the line to continue the story. And then someone else. The actors have to be ready to pick up the story just where it was left off (no repeating words). You can also do this with gibberish (a good way to warm up), sounds, or song.

3-5 minutes.

The Oracle

3-5 actors at a time

The actors create a kind of multi-headed creature, an all-knowing Oracle, by standing close together and linking arms (if you have a big piece of fabric, use it to cover up the actors' bodies to create more of an Oracle effect). One at a time, audience members ask the Oracle a question—about their own lives, the world, etc. After the question has been posed, the Oracle repeats the question (all actors speaking in unison) and then answers the question by one actor speaking one word at a time (starting with the actor stage right), collectively creating sentences and divining the answer to the question. The answer travels down the line a few times until the Oracle feels the answer is complete.

3-5 minutes.

Genre scenes
Small groups

Create performance teams of 4 or 5. Each group picks a fairytale out of a hat—Cinderella, The Three Pigs, Hansel and Gretel, Jack and the Beanstalk, etc. Each group also picks a musical genre out of the hat, e.g., Country, Hard Rock, Rap, or Opera. The groups then have 10 minutes or so to work out how to retell the fairytale through the musical genre that they picked. Each team performs their "musical" for the rest of the group. The performances are 3-5 minutes in length.

Depends on group size.

CROW
Whole group, two at a time

This is an assembly line of giving and taking offers. Standing upstage center, the group forms two vertical lines (each actor faces the back of the next person). Everyone is facing the audience. Line A makes offers; Line B accepts offers. An actor from each line walks downstage center. Actor A offers B a line that will immediately set them in a context and cue as much as possible about character, relationship, whereabouts, etc. An example might be: "Okay, honey, we're lost. I have no idea if the Empire State building is this way or that way." B responds, accepting the offer: "Sweetie, why don't you get out the map?" A responds: "You know I don't believe in maps." And a final line from B: "Babe, that's it. I'm done wondering around this city like lost sheep—I'm going shopping!" After this four-line scene, in which CROW (character, relationship, object, whereabouts) ideally will be established, the two actors join the back of the line in opposite lines (A goes to B line, B rejoins A line). The next two actors come out to start a brand new scene. (Inspired by James Lucal)

10 minutes depending on size of teams.

Moon/mountain

Whole group

The group makes an inner and outer circle. At the cue of the facilitator the two circles move around in opposite directions. When the facilitator cues them to stop, everybody faces a partner from the other circle. The facilitator calls out two characters (first character is for the outer circle and second for the inner circle) and the two actors create a 30 second scene between these two characters. Everybody in the group is doing this simultaneously. After a short exchange, the facilitator cues an ending and the circles begin to move around again until there is a cue to stop and find a new partner. Some examples of characters are: Police officer and teenager; small child and grandmother; more abstractly lust and repulsion; prejudice and justice; the moon and a mountain. (Jonathan Fox)

5 minutes.

Animals

Whole group

This is a great physical warm up as well as a way to create focus in the room. Have everyone lie on their backs (or find a comfortable position with eyes closed). Begin with a short relaxation exercise and then move into a visualization. Invite everybody to go on a journey in their mind's eye, lift up from their bodies, travel through space, over the rooftops and treetops until they land in a beautiful piece of nature. You may have them "explore" the environment a bit and then suggest they sit down somewhere in this environment.

Next, suggest that they hear a sound and when they look over to where the sound came from they see an animal. Invite them to watch this animal for a while—how it moves, what sounds it makes, what it might be doing or looking for—then invite them to step inside this animal's skin and become this animal for a while.... slowly taking the shape of this animal and beginning to move as this creature around the room as accurately as they can. How does the animal walk, fly, or crawl, or slither, how fast or slow, what expression does the animal wear on its face, what sound (if any) does it make? Take time for this transformation and exploration. The various animals in the room might interact.

Eventually, invite the animals to look for any kindred spirits moving about the space. Once you find another animal that seems to belong in your family move around with that animal for a while.

Finally, invite everyone to become still, lie back down and guide the animal spirits to leave the actors' bodies, going back out into the environment from which they came. Perhaps the animal spirit had a message for you. Now guide the actors to journey back in their imagination, out of the place where they "landed," back over the ocean, forest, rooftops, back into the room, back into their own bodies lying on the floor. Allow people to wake up slowly. Finish by sitting in the circle and inviting people to share what animal they were and the message the animal left with them (optional).

15 minutes.

Animal scenes

Two people at a time

The two actors up are assigned two different animals, taking on the qualities of those animals but remaining human. Then they are given the who, where, and what. So it might be a snake-like person interviewing a sloth-like person for a job. Or a horse-like person and a parrot-like person are meeting up on a first Internet date. After the characters and circumstances are assigned, the two actors improvise the scene. A great exercise to follow the Animal exercise. (Steve and Carole Ford)

5 minutes.

Hitchhiker

Teams

Set up the chairs on stage as if four seats in a car. Two actors take the front seat; one is driving. Make up a scenario for them: father/son taking a drive; married couple coming back from dinner; adult mother taking elderly father food shopping. This first scene runs for a couple of minutes. Another actor picks a card from the hat, giving her a physical or emotional condition that this actor has to take on. (Examples: bad case of poison ivy; extremely absent minded; nervous twitch; extremely upset, angry, or frightened; bad case of giggles, etc.) She enters the stage as a hitchhiker, sticking out her thumb. The people driving the car pick up the hitchhiker, find out where she is going, make small talk, etc. The hitchhiker continues to enact her "condition" while making small talk. Slowly but surely the characters in front catch on to what her condition is. It is their task, in character, logically, to find a reason to also take on this condition. The objective is reached when everyone in the car has caught on and is twitching, very angry, or scratching like mad.

2 minutes each scene.

Landmark

Whole group

Paper and pen

Invite people to reflect on the big landmark moments or experiences of their lives so far. When they are ready, they choose five to sketch/draw these on paper. They can draw these moments as points on a life map if they wish. Then they choose one of these moments and do some journaling on this experience--trying to recall all of the details. Finally, people are invited to share this landmark life experience as a solo piece, which will involve using words and movement.

20-30 minutes depending on size of group.

In the manner of the word

Whole group

One person goes out of the room. The rest of the group thinks of an adverb (e.g., gracefully, joyously, stealthily). The person comes back in and tries to guess the selected word by giving group members scene assignments, instructing people to do things "in the manner of the word." If the word is "elegantly," the person may ask two people to "dance in the manner of the word." They stand and dance as elegantly as they can. Then the person may ask another person to make peanut butter and jelly sandwiches "in the manner of the word." She may ask the whole group to brush their teeth "in the manner of the word." She continues assigning scenes until she has guessed the word. I often have two people go out at a time, and they work in tandem to try to guess the word.

10 minutes

Elements

Small groups

Each group chooses one of the four elements (earth, wind, fire and air) and then creates a mini-performance piece about it. These performances can go in any direction: a literal story or abstract piece of dance/theatre. If there are props or fabric or instruments they can be incorporated in the piece. Groups are given 10-15 minutes to rehearse and then perform their five-minute pieces in front of each other. You can also use the seasons or any other theme as a starting point.

20 minutes.

Closing Activities

Wish for the world

Whole group

Pass a ball or symbolic object around the circle and ask people to share a "Wish for the World."

Depends on size of group.

Next step sculptures

Groups of 3-5

This is a useful exercise towards the end of a workshop or series of classes. In small groups, each person "sculpts" her/his *next step* (in terms of learning Playback or in terms of a specific question posed in class or after college, etc.). The other actors are "clay" and the sculptor positions them (either through physical touch or demonstration—there is no talking) into a still, silent image of her own next step. The sculptor does not need to use everybody in her group. She places herself in the sculpture and thinks up a title for her stage picture, which she keeps to herself for now. The group members remember their roles and place in each picture and the next person in the group sculpts his next step.

At the end, the group moves seamlessly and silently through each person's image, creating a kind of slideshow. Depending on how many people are in each group you leave about 15 minutes for this part. When all the images are made, each team displays the images for the rest of the group by cycling through the images. For each one, the sculptor (who is in the picture) says the title, the group holds the picture for another beat and then transitions to the next picture. It is nice for a musician to play during the slideshows, accenting each picture/next step.

20 minutes.

Lullaby

Partners

In dyads, invite each person to sing a lullaby to her/his partner. The "lullaby" can be any song sung gently. Depending on the comfort level in the group, you may want to "hold" your partner while you sing, or have the listener put her head on your lap. This is a nice way to end a session, especially if it has been particularly emotional. (Jo Salas)

8-10 minutes.

High five

Whole group

Another quick way to end a session is to pass around the high-five, standing in a circle. It is fun to have people say "high-five" or "hey" or "good job!" as they high-five each other.

Depends on group size; 1 minute.

Appreciation circle

Whole group

Sitting or standing in a circle each person appreciates something specific about the person to the left (or right). These appreciations are said out loud for the whole group to hear.

1 minute per person.

Behind your back

Groups of three

One person in the triad turns his back to the other two.

They begin to have a conversation about the person with his back turned, talking about him in strictly positive terms, appreciating certain qualities about who he is and/or moments from his work in the class. The subject simply sits with his back turned and listens/ absorbs the positive feedback and reflection!

4 minutes per person.

Pass the squeeze-with sound

Whole group

Otherwise known as "Electricity." This is a nice way to start or end a session. The group members hold hands, eyes closed. One person squeezes one of the hands she's holding, and this person, in turn, squeezes the next person's hand. A current of electricity moves around the circle. You can encourage the current to move faster, like lightning down a rod. Finally, you can invite people to make a small sound as the electricity passes through them, so the circle will come alive with spontaneous sounds. Eventually, someone is invited to "swallow" the motion to end the game.

3 minutes.

Closing clap

Whole group

As a group, you come up with a word, or maybe you just use "hah!" Everyone in the circle raises their left hand and, on a count of three (you can decide to count forward or backwards, in English or in another language) everyone brings their left hand to meet their right with a clap, saying the designated word in unison. This is a clear, clean, quick way to end a session or a workshop.

Everyone needs to know that once the clap has happened, the session is over! (Matt Chapman)

30 seconds.

Appendix A

Warm up sequences for Playback Theatre forms

The art of teaching Playback Theatre is beyond the scope of this book, but if you are someone who is already knowledgeable about Playback, here are some warm up sequences for Playback Theatre forms that I have found effective. Please see page 128 for more explanation about Playback Theatre and relevant resources.

Stories

Chorus 94

Three part story 93

Closing activities

Appendix B

Exercises especially effective with youth

(Listed in no particular order)

Working with young people is a privilege—and can also be challenging. The exercises and games need to meet their energy as well as resonate with their level of life experience and therefore must be explained in clear, relevant language. Below is a list of exercises I have found especially effective with youth (listed in no particular order).

Appendix C

Notes about some influential disciplines

Action Theatre, created by Ruth Zaporah, is an improvisational physical theatre method used in both workshop and performance, in which performers explore the connections between body, voice, story, and ensemble through spontaneous play. Zaporah's work has been widely practiced for decades and has influenced many practitioners.

Action Theater: The Improvisation Of Presence, Ruth Zaporah
www.actiontheater.com

Contact Improvisation, created originally by Steve Paxton (and developed by Nancy Stark Smith, Lisa Nelson, and others), is an improvisation dance technique in which dancers move in and out of physical contact with one another: giving and receiving weight, lifting, rolling, falling, leaning, carrying and catching. In CI we are given the opportunity to tune in and listen to another person or group of dancers very deeply, through the body, without speaking, and are forced to stay in the present moment as each dancer follows inner impulses to move. In CI we dance in duets, groups and sometimes on our own.

www.contactquarterly.com

Motion Theater, created by Nina Wise, is a form of improvisational physical storytelling in which participants access memories through movement and then embody and articulate fragments of these life experiences using movement and text simultaneously. Motion Theater uses very specific language, grounded in the present tense, that focuses on the poetic detail of our life stories, rather than general or sentimental reporting. There are many excellent physical and vocal warm up exercises connected to this method.

A Big New Free Happy Unusual Life: Self-Expression and Spiritual Practice for Those Who Have Time for Neither, Nina Wise
www.ninawise.com

Playback Theatre was conceived in 1975 by Jonathan Fox and developed together with his wife, Jo Salas, and the original Playback Theatre company. In Playback, audience members volunteer life stories, which actors enact on stage. Playback Theatre's aims are to make good theatre as well as to create a space for community stories to be heard. Playback Theatre ultimately effects positive social change through dialogue and by generating empathy.

Improvising Real Life: Personal story in Playback Theatre, Jo Salas

Acts of Service: Spontaneity, Commitment, Tradition in the Nonscripted Theatre, Jonathan Fox
www.playbackcentre.org
www.bigappleplayback.com

Psychodrama, created by J. L. Moreno and later developed by his wife, Zerka Moreno, is a therapeutic method that uses dramatic action and role-playing in group settings to work through individual and group issues. In psychodrama people enact life dramas on stage, playing themselves, and group members play other key characters. Sociometry, a related method, makes connections between group members visible, often by exploring them through action.

Focus on Psychodrama: the Therapeutic Aspects of Psychodrama, Peter Kellerman.

The Essential Moreno: Writings on Psychodrama, Group Method, and Spontaneity by J.L. Moreno, MD, Jonathan Fox, Ed.
www.asgpp.org

Theatre of the Oppressed, created by Brazilan director Augusto Boal, is an expansive set of political theatre structures, including Forum Theatre, Rainbow of Desire, Invisible Theatre, Newspaper Theatre, Legislative Theatre and Image Theatre. T.O. strives to use theatre as a "rehearsal for the future" and arm its participants with the strength and confidence to face social and personal (relationship) issues. Most popular among its structures is Forum Theatre in which actors make theatre around community issues and audience members (called "spectactors") enter the scene on stage by making suggestions through action. Boal has also given us copious amounts of terrific theatre games, which I use readily in my work.

Theatre of the Oppressed, Augusto Boal

Games For Actors and Non-Actors, Augusto Boal

Viewpoints is an ensemble-building and composition technique created by director Ann Bogart. Bogart and her colleagues have created nine "viewpoints" for actors to consider when working together. The viewpoints are divided into two main subject areas: time and space. Bogart was inspired by choreographer Mary Overlie who is credited for "discovering" the first six viewpoints in the 1970s. I find Viewpoints especially helpful in generating focus, body-awareness, and forcing us to make clean, clear, committed choices on stage.

The Viewpoints Book: A Practical Guide to Viewpoints and Composition, Anne Bogart and Tina Landau
www.siti.org

APPENDIX D

THE POWER SHUFFLE

The Power Shuffle exercise is a diversity awareness activity that asks us to explore issues of identity and to examine how the power structure is set up in the United States (but you can adjust questions for other societies) in terms of rank and privilege. This exercise can stir things up so it is important to set it up carefully and definitely leave time afterward for discussion. (It works very well to follow this exercise with Playback.) The facilitator needs to have put considerable time and commitment into exploring her own life and feelings about privilege, racism, and diversity.

Generally speaking, in the USA, anyway, certain aspects of identity are associated with power: being white, male, middle or owning class, Christian, educated, able-bodied, etc. Everyone else has less access to employment opportunities, education, health care and other resources. This exercise opens up an opportunity to understand some of these power differentials. With the exception of the facilitator's words, this activity is done in silence. Usually, I follow the exercise by asking people to get into small groups (4 or 5) to discuss their experience, and consider the debrief questions. There are many versions of the Power Shuffle (or Diversity Shuffle) out there; and you can make your own. The following explanation I took from *Transforming Communities* website, www.transformcommunities.org.

> In this exercise, participants are invited to self-identify as

*belonging to various social groups by performing an action that sets them apart from others. The facilitator may want to suggest some ground rules, or ask participants to create group agreements, related to respecting individual members' experience and preserving confidentiality. Facilitators should also take care to point out at the start of the exercise that participation is **voluntary**. Group members should be informed that they do **not** have to identify themselves as belonging to any particular group or category if they don't wish to reveal that information about themselves. This exercise should only be used by experienced facilitators who are comfortable with helping people process strong reactions in a group setting. If this exercise does not feel safe for your group, it's best to omit it.*

The facilitator asks group participants to stand on one side of the room. For each prompt people will be crossing to the other side of the room, turning around to face group members who didn't walk, looking to see who did walk, and then walking back across the room to join the rest of the group. I find that it is good to make sure the journey across isn't too vast, in other words, use the narrowest part of the room for the crossing space if possible. For each category, people can decide for themselves whether to walk or not, and each category is up to each person's interpretation. For each category, the facilitator says:

"Please cross to the other side of the room if you are..."
(insert category from list below)

"Notice who's standing with you . . . notice who's not."

"Notice how it feels."

"Cross back and join the rest of the group."

Categories (this version taken from www.amsa.org):

You are a woman.

You are Asian, East Asian, South Asian/Indian, or Pacific Islander.

You are Latino/a, Chicano/a, or mestizo/a.

You are of Arabian descent.

You are Native American or at least one of your parents is full-blooded Native American.

You are African-American or black, or of African descent.

You are of multi-heritage, and at least one of your parents or grandparents is a person of color.

You are of Jewish heritage.

You are 45 or over.

You are under 21 (or pick another appropriate age for the group).

You were raised poor.

You were raised by a single parent or currently are a single parent.

One of your parents, or the people who raised you, were or are working-class and did manual labor, skilled or unskilled work, or pink-collar clerical or service work to make a living.

You were raised in an isolated or farming community.

Neither of your parents, or the people who raised you, attended college (or received a college degree).

You were raised Catholic.

You have a visible or hidden physical disability or impairment.

You have ever been seriously or continually sick.

You are an immigrant to this country.

Your native language is other than English.

You come from a family where alcohol or drugs were or are a problem.

You were raised in or are now part of a religious community other than Christian.

You are lesbian, gay, bisexual, or transgender. (Always decide whether it is safe enough to call out this category and don't be overcautious; if no one walks across, you can point out the lack of safety in the group later.)

Someone in your family, or a close friend, is lesbian, gay, bisexual or transgender.

You are a non-management worker and/or do not supervise anyone on your job.

You are now or ever have been unemployed, not by choice.

You are a veteran.

You or a member of your family has ever been labeled mentally ill or crazy.

You or a member of your family have ever been incarcerated or been in the juvenile justice system.

You were ever publicly labeled fat, whether or not you ever felt fat.

Other categories may be added as appropriate, and some of these can be deleted depending upon the composition of the group, the issues to be covered, and the amount of time available.

Possible debrief questions:

1. How did it feel to be in the group which walked across?

2. How did it feel to watch others cross?

3. What feelings came up for you during the exercise?

4. Did you walk a little or a lot? How do you feel about that?

5. What surprised you during this exercise?

6. Other thoughts, feelings or comments.

If you're doing the Power Shuffle in the context of a Playback Theatre workshop, this is a great time to use some action. Rotating teams can reflect comments and responses in fluid sculptures and other short forms. You might want to give everyone a chance to debrief verbally first in small groups or with a partner for a few minutes first, especially if the group is large, and then go into Playback forms.

Power shuffle resources:

www.amsa.org
www.transformcommunities.org
www.hunterhouse.com

REFERENCES

Boal, Augusto. *Games for Actors and Non-actors.* 2nd edition. New York: Routledge, 2003.

Bogart, Anne and Landau, Tina. *The Viewpoints Book: A Practical Guide to Viewpoints and Composition.* New York: Theatre Communications Group, Inc. 2005.

Fox, Hannah. "Playback Theatre." *Interactive and Improvisational Drama: Varieties of Applied Theatre and Performance.* Adam Blatner, Ed. Lincoln, NE: iUniverse, 2007.

Fox, Hannah. "Playback Theatre: Inciting Dialogue and Building Community through Personal Story." *The Drama Review.* 51.4 (2007): 89-105.

Fox, Jonathan. *Acts of Service: Spontaneity, Commitment, Tradition in the Nonscripted Theatre.* New Paltz, NY: Tusitala Publishing, 1994.

Fox, Jonathan and Dauber, Heinrich. (Eds.) *Gathering Voices: Essays on Playback Theatre.* New Paltz, NY: Tusitala Publishing, 1999.

Iyengar, B.K.S. *Light on Yoga.* New York: Schocken, 1977.

Johnstone, Keith. *Impro: Improvisation and the Theatre.* London: Eyre Methuen Ltd, 1981.

Linklater, Kristin. *Freeing the Natural Voice.* New York: Drama Publishers, 1976.

Nachmanovitch, Stephen. *Free Play: Improvisation in Life and Art.* New York: Tarcher/Penguin, 1990.

Rohd, Michael. *Theatre for Community, Conflict & Dialogue.* Portsmouth, NH: Heinemann, 1998.

Salas, Jo *Improvising Real Life: Personal Story in Playback Theatre.* Dubuque, IA: Kendall/Hunt, 1993.

Spolin, Viola. *Improvisation for the Theater.* 3rd edition. Evanston: Northwestern University Press, 1999.

Wise, Nina. *A Big Free Happy Unusual Life.* New York: Broadway Books, 2002.

Zaporah, Ruth. *Action Theater: Improvisation of Presence.* Berkeley; North Atlantic Books, 1995.

Relevant websites:

Centre for Playback Theatre: www.playbackcentre.org

International Playback Theatre Network: www.playbacknet.org

Big Apple Playback Theatre: www.bigappleplayback.com

Training for Change: www.trainingforchange.org

Siti Company (Ann Bogart): www.siti.org

Contact Improvisation publications and workshops: www.contactquarterly.com

Acknowledgements

I would like to acknowledge my drama teachers: Steve and Carole Ford, Deb Margolin, Augusto Boal, Helen White, Chris Vine, Lenora Champagne, Judith Sloan, Richard Schechner, Marc Weinblatt, Nina Wise, Lola Broomberg, Robin Aronson, Frances Batten, Enid Lefton, Eugene Playback Theatre, Big Apple Playback Theatre, my students, and my parents, Jo Salas and Jonathan Fox.

ABOUT THE AUTHOR

Hannah Fox is a professor of dance and theatre at Manhattanville College. She is artistic director of Big Apple Playback Theatre based in New York City. Hannah teaches dance, theatre, and improv workshops internationally.